THE TELLER
OF TALL TALES

THE TELLER
OF TALL TALES

A novel by
Michael Henry Birch

ELF PUBLISHING COMPANY

Elf Publishing Company
Langton Villa Langton Green
Royal Tunbridge Wells
TN3 0BB England
Fax: 0892 511 110

A CIP catalogue record of this book is
available from the British Library

ISBN 1 872900 05 4

This book was written, printed and finished using
SELF-PUBLISHING SYSTEMS technology

By the author

Novels The Teller of Tall Tales
The Death of Pinocchio
Dark Corners

Short Stories Like Some People Do
Suspended Tales

Poetry Cursory Rhymes (Satirical Verses)
My Head On The Line And Mad Doggerel

In memory of Marguerite and Louis

*I gratefully acknowledge Janet Birch's
important creative contribution to this book*
M.H.B

"Tell me, are these tales true?"
"Ah, my friend, they would surely
be true if I were someone else"

Hassan el Telmisani
Tales of Innocence

CONTENTS

The Travelling Teller Of Tales

The little boy was six years old and he lived with his mother and father in a village some miles down the coast from the town of Alexandria in Egypt. The village was so small that it didn't have a name — in fact it was not much more than a few houses and shops, a small convent, a Bedouin settlement, and a tram stop along the coastal section of track.

The tram stop had been named *'Palais'* because it was close to a palace built on a hill overlooking the Mediterranean coast. An enigmatic sister of King Fuad and her retinue of servants dwelt in that large bleak building, with its turrets and faded pink exterior and permanently closed shutters. The princess had reputedly been consigned to her isolated existence because she was mad. In another version of the story, it was because she had fallen in love with a most unsuitable person against the king's wishes.

All the little boy knew about her was that one late afternoon, after catching sight of him boldly helping himself to a ripe pomegranate in her orchard, she had greeted him with extreme courtesy, invited him to join her on the terrace facing the sea and offered him a cup of Turkish coffee, some Turkish Delights containing pistachio nuts, and a Turkish cigarette that he accepted and later smoked in secret.

She had green eyes, long jet black hair, a gold tooth, thin crimson-purple painted lips and a very white complexion.

She smelt of jasmine and did not appear mad to the enchanted child as she gently asked him questions about himself while they watched the sun setting.

Yes, now it all seems so very clear. I believe that sixty years ago I may have been that boy.

Why yes, I remember other things too. . . that I was the only European child in the area. And that down the road, not far from our bungalow, there was that small group of houses and shops opposite the convent of Notre Dame Du Sacré Coeur Sanglant de Jésus. The emblem on the convent's wrought iron gates was a large crimson heart crowned with a gilded halo of thorns. There were drops of blood painted in a darker shade of red where the heart was pierced by a thorn.

There was Madame Mimi Ferguson, a Maltese lady who lived in the big old house behind our villa with her husband Mr Jock Ferguson, a Scottish engineer who, my father had told me, *built* canals. Which, he had added thoughtfully, is not the same as *digging* them. Madame Mimi was a very large lady of nervous disposition. I only mention her state of nerves because I remember that on the rare occasions when I visited her to ask if I could pick some of the ripe medlars from the tree in her garden, she used to let out a startled cry of surprise if I addressed her when her back was turned. Even if I spoke very quietly and she knew I was in the same room.

I also remember that she used to wash a plucked chicken with carbolic soap in warm water before cooking it. She must have enjoyed doing that very much because she would hum contentedly as she worked up a frothy lather, scrubbing it into the crevices and round the limbs. She would then rinse the chicken under the tap and place it on its back on a clean towel where she would dry it with all the tender care of. . . but no, there is no point in my continuing. . . it is surely quite sufficient to say that the sight of a plucked chicken still troubles me to this day.

To our left, there was a villa designed and built by a young architect whose name was Ezzedine Omar and occupied by him and his wife whose name was Baby. At least, that's what he called her, and so everyone called her that too, except the servants who respectfully called her 'Ya sitte Baby', which means 'Mrs Baby' in Arabic. He was tall and thin and she was short and plump and very cuddly. They had planned the arrival of their first child, as yet unconceived, with meticulous and extravagantly loving care.

I remember Baby and Ezzedine showing my parents and me round the suite of rooms that he had designed for the prospective child. Everything was built to a mini scale: the bedroom, the bathroom, the custom-made furniture and tiny fittings, even the doors. . . all intended to accommodate a child between the ages of, say, seven and ten, or, as it struck my stirred-up mind at the time, perhaps the travelling dwarf who sold ice-cream in crisp pink cornets from the large brass tub he carried on his back. Anyway, I had found it all quite fascinating. The ceilings were so low that an adult had to bend over. I was briefly in my perfect element, surrounded by four grown-ups bowing low in my presence. It would, of course, not have occurred to me to wonder what would happen when the child eventually grew too large for its miniature home, because I had given no thought at that time to ever growing up. It was not until many years later, long after we had moved away to Cairo, that I discovered that the problem had not arisen because Baby had only ever had one baby, and that it had not survived.

And across the road to our right, there was a two storey house that belonged to a Pasha. He was a Cabinet Minister whose senior wife, a European lady, resided there. It had a three-tiered timber tower rising from the roof, constructed in the style of a small pagoda, and which seemed to serve no useful purpose other than as a roost and nesting spot for wild doves. I remember expressing to our gardener Mahroos my eager desire to go and live up there with the birds, for a while at any rate, until he pointed out to me that I may find the smelly accretion of droppings not entirely to my taste.

A desire of a different kind, however, was easily satisfied every day when I slaked my thirst from the garden tap that received its untreated water supply from the nearest canal. Canal water owed its murky brown ochre colour and unusual flavour to the fact that it was enriched not only by nutritious Nile silt, but also with a variety of decomposing organic matter that was regularly dumped into it. This included raw sewage as well as the bloated corpses of, among other creatures, dogs, sheep, oxen, donkeys, and the occasional human, all of which could be observed floating past if one stood on the canal bank for long enough. It was the perfect breeding medium for deadly micro-organisms and parasites of every kind.

On reflection, I now realize that drinking that toxic fermentation would either kill you off in due course, or, as in my case, enable you to develop a life-long immunity to virtually every known infection. Curiously enough, the garden tap water was not redolent of the revolting things I have just described. . . on the contrary, it tasted fresh and cool to me, and it had a fragrantly earthy bouquet. In fact, as I recall, it was more pleasant than the clear featureless tepid stuff that came out of the kitchen faucet.

The wall surrounding that mysterious property across the road was very high, like a fortress, and although I had sometimes heard children's voices on the other side, I only

once caught a glimpse through the bars of the main gate of
two little girls wearing black velvet dresses and patent
leather shoes as they ran down the marble steps of the
house into a large black and crimson limousine. I never saw
them again. I remember being told by my mother that they
were going to school in Switzerland, which was another
country far away across the sea where there were mountains
and snow. I was puzzled at the time because it did not seem
all that practicable to travel so far just to go to school,
unless school was terribly important of course. But I had
no way of knowing, and besides, I had never seen
mountains or snow.

The only person on that property whom I observed
regularly as I strolled past the gates was their Nubian
gardener. He was young, exceedingly tall and black, and he
would periodically display his erection, of which he seemed
rather proud in a detached and dignified sort of way, to us
local children. He would now and then, if he was in the
right frame of mind, allow us the privilege of venturing into
a corner of the garden where he would watch solemnly as
one of the little Arab girls in our wide-eyed group prodded
the object inquisitively and briefly with her finger. He
would then tuck it away out of sight and that was all there
was to it. The boys tended to keep their distance, but we
were all no doubt lastingly impressed.

Across the road from the south end of our garden lived the
Bedouin family community of Abu Bakr with his many
wives, his unmarried sons and daughters, his older sons
with their rather fewer wives, their children, lots of
grand-children, and a few elderly relatives, some of whom
were very ancient and, in some cases, a trifle eccentric.

There was the widow Mabrooka, for instance, well into her
seventies, who continued to dye her hair and the palms of
her hands with henna and to blacken her eyes with kohl, a

little carelessly perhaps, because her eyes never seemed quite symmetrical. She would smirk seductively at male visitors and make startling erotic overtures to them that would have earned a much younger woman a roar of threatening disapproval from old Abu Bakr. Unlike the young women, Mabrooka seemed under no obligation to wear the loose black robes that screened them from head to toe from the gaze of male outsiders, leaving only a narrow slit for their dark eyes to peer through.

And there was Ibn Mahmood, another elder, whose appointed duty it was to slaughter, in the proper ceremonial manner, every animal destined for the cooking pot. This meant chopping the heads off chickens and slitting the jugular veins of sheep with such skill that the animal would be drained of almost all its blood before expiring. The strangest thing of all, and which I recall most vividly, is that Ibn Mahmood would place his hand gently on the sheep's head and whisper words in its ear, words that I could not overhear. But they had the effect of quietening the poor beast as its life burst out of its neck in a bright crimson jet. Although the cooked flesh would, it was said, be lighter in colour and more palatable, the method of slaughter was not, in fact, a matter of choice but of obedience to a strict ordinance of their religion.

On those occasions, his wife, Om Khalif, would be standing by with a beaker of fresh goat milk and a glass tumbler that she would hold by the docile animal's throat and half fill from the small fountain of blood. She would then fill the glass to the top with milk from the beaker and hand it to Abu Bakr who would drain it in one gulp. She would repeat the process and hand the glass to other males who would sip a mouthful before passing the pink beverage on to another member of the family. No one ever spoke while all this took place. Abu Bakr once handed the full glass to me with a smile and told me to drink it all. I did. It was warm and slightly sweet. I remember, too, that I received a round of applause from all the family. I was six years old and felt, proudly, that I had been initiated as a fully-fledged member of that exclusive Bedouin community.

Ibn Mahmood would always complete his gruesome task by severing the sheep's head with the maximum of dramatic panache and with obvious relish, flashing his bloody knife and leaping about while crying out his thanks to Allah for His Munificence. He would then skin and gut the carcass and toss the innards to the pariah dogs who would fight savagely over the prize before swallowing the torn fragments of entrails. It would all be over in moments. We children would watch the whole grisly affair from start to finish with morbid fascination, and Ibn Mahmood's bizarre behaviour was all the more disconcertingly impressive to us children because at all other times he was one of the quietest and most docile members of the family.

Abu Bakr — the name means Father Buffalo — was the founding father and head of the community. He was a tall and erect man with a large moustache, and always carried a nabboot, the long straight wooden stave that is not only the traditional weapon of the Bedouin male but also the instrument of sporting contests and of ritual dances. Many are the skulls that have been cracked down the centuries with a firm blow from a nabboot. It is also not surprising that 'nabboot' should be the vulgar and prideful name for the male erection.

The community had grown considerably since the day that the young Abu Bakr had ventured out of his desert homeland. He had travelled a great distance and finally pitched his tent on that parcel of waste land beside the tram tracks and settled down there with his first bride to start a dynasty.

His descendants had, over the years, built their small
dwellings with sun-dried mud bricks and corrugated iron
roofs around the larger whitewashed house that had
eventually replaced the tent, and that was now occupied by
Abu Bakr and his younger wives.

The older wives, some quite elderly by then, either lived
peacefully on their own in adjoining dwellings, having
acquitted themselves of their wifely duties over the years,
or, if they were not quite so old, shared their
accommodation with their nubile daughters, where they
periodically received the occasional connubial visit from
the old buffalo, who was always mindful of their needs as
he saw fit.

By the time I appeared on that scene I must have been
about four years old. My mother, I should explain, was
French, fair haired, small, very attractive, and her name was
Marguerite. She had been a professional singer with a
touring variety company, until the manager absconded with
the takings and left the artistes stranded and penniless in
Alexandria.

Not long after that contretemps she met my father, a quiet
English gentleman with impeccable manners who wore
pince-nez and who fell instantly in love with her and
remained so for the rest of his life, and who, moreover,
always addressed her as 'vous', instead of the intimate 'tu',
to the very day he died at the age of eighty-seven. She was
of even more nervous disposition than Madame Mimi
Ferguson with whom she did not get on too well on account
of the fact that the good lady did not consider my mother
to be an entirely respectable person because of her
connection with the theatre. At least that was what my
mother told me about forty years later.

I mention my mother's state of nerves for two reasons: the
first is that they played a large part in my life for half a

century, and the second reason is that, looking back to those early days, it now seems strange to me that she did not appear to fret over my frequent disappearances from home for whole days at a time to be with my Bedouin friends.

On the other hand, when I was within her field of vision, she would work herself into a state of panic at the thought that I might trip over some obstacle, fall down, fracture my skull and die before her very eyes. She would sometimes describe the imaginary dreadful scene in detail to me. And it was *excessivement pénible* for her, as she put it, especially since it had been her choice that I was to be her only child. Besides, the whole inelegant business of conceiving, carrying, and then giving birth to me had been painful and, moreover, singularly lacking in finesse, even though I was an uniquely beautiful baby, as she also confided to me some forty years later. In any event, she had not been inclined to go through all that again, she added, not even to please my father for whom she always had a great deal of love and respect.

She obviously cared a great deal about my safety and well-being, because she was always screaming *'attention!'* at me. This sometimes resulted in my accidentally walking straight into pieces of furniture which, of course, was quite painful and made me cry a lot. That would make her even more nervous. My mother died at the age of eighty-four when she was struck down by a speeding motorcyclist while crossing the road. That was *excessivement pénible* for me. Especially as I had recently got into the habit of saying *'Fais bien attention Maman'* to her.

By the time I was five, I was sharing almost full time in the life of the Abu Bakr community and my parents seemed to be reconciled to my going barefoot and wearing a ghallabeya, which is the plain robe worn by native Arabs and Bedouins. I also spoke their language, ate their food, and more often than not slept with their children on a rush mat in their homes.

When my father took me on his fortnightly visit to his widowed mother, I would be scrubbed and dressed in a velvet suit that smelt of mothballs. My grandmother smelt of lavender eau de cologne and mothballs, so I don't suppose it mattered much. She was ninety years old, with very pale blue eyes, all her own teeth, and she had an exceptionally calm disposition.

Once, on one of our visits, she noticed that I had fallen into the garden pond and that only my hat could be seen floating on the surface. Not wishing to interrupt my father, she had waited thoughtfully until he had finished his sentence before pointing out to him that I may be in some kind of difficulty. My father, I was told many years later, handed his pince-nez to her before plunging in to fish me out. His family were, without a doubt, not easily ruffled.

My mother did not accompany us on those visits because, as I discovered when I was too old to do anything about it, everyone assumed that Grandmama, like Madame Mimi Ferguson, may not have considered Marguerite an entirely respectable person to entertain in her home.

Yet, considering that one of my paternal uncles was known to have had a long-lasting and, according to family legend, a somewhat flagrant affair with his Indian coachman and that another uncle was a manic alcoholic who had compromised the family's honour with some embarrassingly dubious business ventures — and that is not to mention the extra-marital adventures and the various scandals in which close friends of my father's family were involved — the grounds for ostracizing my mother were a little hard for her to appreciate. But this was all beyond my knowledge at the time.

Besides, there were other things on my mind. There were the daily swims in the ocean: even now I shudder at the thought of my mother's frantic reaction if she had seen me thrashing about joyfully and alone in the often rough and dangerous surf beating onto that deserted beach. There was the occasional Bedouin wedding to attend, and the periodic exorcism of demonic spirits from the body of a young woman to observe.

The possessed victim would be draped from head to foot in a white veil and made to dance round and round a column of palm fronds bedecked with lit candles, sometimes for a whole day and night. A travelling shaman would all the while be chanting magical verses monotonously to chase the demons away, while the woman's close family, standing in a circle, took it in turn to clap their hands slowly in unison for hours on end. The woman would continue her rotations in a trance until at last she would give a loud and prolonged scream and fall to the ground in a violent fit, her limbs flailing the ground and the froth from her mouth bubbling through the thin fabric covering her face. She would then fall into a deep sleep and be carried to her room by the womenfolk who would wash and perfume her. The next day, the young woman would be going about her chores as though nothing had happened.

Then there was always the stalking and chasing off of the large number of feral cats that preyed on chickens and tame pigeons that were an important source of the community's livelihood. There were visits to the shoemaker, whose shop smelt of leather and beeswax, and who always let us watch him cobbling shoes with soles made from sections cut out of old motor tyres. There was the tram station, where we would sometimes get a free ride to the next station if the conductor was Abu Bakr's son Habib. Watching the convent girls at play and pulling funny faces at them was good for a little light entertainment, until we were chased away by the supervising nun, which would be an added divertissement.

And there were the toys we made for ourselves from small pieces of wood given to us by the local carpenter; from fabric and strips of leather; from seashells, nutshells, bits of scrap metal, coloured yarn — anything we could lay our hands on. The boys made and dressed as many little dolls as did the girls, and the girls were as bold and adventurous as the boys when it came to doing forbidden things — like trespassing into the Princess's garden, and fearfully and furtively climbing the steep and narrow wooden staircase to the furnished hut nestling high up in the crotch of an enormous banyan tree. And then examining in bewilderment, among other things, the set of Tarot cards and the postcards, the ones with pictures of nuns with naked men wearing top hats and socks with suspenders, and those of two naked women, and of two men and one woman, all performing strange acts — those cards were secreted in the drawer of a small escritoire that had inlays in ivory and mother of pearl in the shape of flowers. We never stole anything, but the temptation to do so was sometimes very hard to resist because there was a large number of glittering and valuable little objects on display in that royal personage's arboreal folly and they belonged to another world that existed beyond our childish imaginings. We did, however, keep our eyes open for any gentlemen wearing top hats in the vicinity of the convent. . . for a short while at any rate, until we tired of the fruitless vigil.

But the high spot in our lives was the periodic arrival of the Travelling Teller of Tales. The adults were as thrilled as the children by the appearance of this entertainer. He was a one-man repertory company, a dispenser of fantasy, a familiar with those spirits that conjure up exotic tales, and also the weaver of old yarns with such skill that they always seemed new and could still fill one with the surprises of the unexpected. He would be treated with the awe-struck deference accorded to the stars of stage and screen in places far away.

Soon after his arrival he would be offered delicacies and strong tea prepared by the women and he would eat and sip daintily and silently, every mouthful taken being avidly watched by most members of the family. This was, in a way, a warming up for the actual performance that would come later. He would be showing us that he was little more than the humble wanderer, right now in the daylight, in contrast to the mysterious Teller of Tales who would be possessed with all the faces and voices of the characters in the stories into which he would be transporting us after the sun had set.

The small amphitheatre of dim light created by a few paraffin lamps would then enclose his audience and isolate them from the world outside as he would spin his words into our heads and suspend all disbelief in the unlikely, in the implausible and in the impossible. Shadows would lengthen, sounds would take on different meanings, and dimensions would become part of that other reality.

He would start with a few hilarious short anecdotes involving a favourite traditional character, the indomitable Goha, that perennial innocent who always triumphed in the end over the rich, the powerful and foolishly rapacious antagonists who, until just before the final punch line, appeared to have the advantage over him. These were tales that concluded with an ironic twist and which would unfailingly draw loud laughter and applause from an audience that had already primed itself emotionally to yield to total enjoyment. If I allowed myself to exaggerate a little, I would now be saying that nothing short of a cosmic cataclysm could possibly have interrupted that resolve, so determined were we all to feast ourselves on this man's hypnotic performance. But I must not damn him with overpraise.

He would then follow, in complete contrast, with a long tale filled with dramatic events, dark deeds and violent passions, murder and mayhem, and spiced with magical happenings and with romance. As he would be approaching the climax of the action, when imminent danger was about to overtake the heroic protagonist, the Teller of Tales would mischievously digress into some tedious irrelevancy, some exasperating descriptions of trivial details, while feigning ignorance of the very perilous situation into which he had plunged our imagination.

The suspense would become intolerable, we would be screaming our warnings. Having led us to the brink, he would then, with perfect timing, suddenly find a way to rescue our hero and at the same time to liberate the tension he had so carefully built up, and we would all burst out laughing.

That man standing before us could make us hold our breath in concert, and then with a single gesture or with a few words make us release it either with our cries of vicarious fear or through our sighs of relief. . . and this with stories that we had heard many times before. His repertoire of tales may or may not have been fathomless, I had no way of knowing, but the telling was always infinitely varied.

Sometimes he would start with a familiar adventure story, add a fresh character who would drive him wildly into a whole new impromptu tale. This appeared, alarmingly, to lead him into a labyrinthine plot, or even into a narrative dead end that then required all his skill as a story-teller to escape from, while avoiding confusing his audience, and worse, from losing his tight hold on their attention.

Often, when he was telling a story and also acting the parts, it appeared to me, watching him with total absorption, that the Teller of Tales had somehow turned into several palpable characters simultaneously and that their dialogue was actually overlapping when they interrupted one another. The man moved with rapid gestures at times and in slow motion at others, and then he would seem to be moving rapidly and slowly at the same time. He would speak in a whisper so that we could barely hear what he was saying and he would unexpectedly shriek the next bit of dialogue, throwing his audience into shock. He would then calm us again with crooning sounds that had no direct meaning, before resuming his narrative.

He would occasionally pause in silence and shake his head over the irrational or incorrigible actions of one of his characters, raise his arms skyward and look up imploringly, and then he would turn to us and shrug his shoulders as though that character's perverse conduct was so far beyond his comprehension that we would have to explain it to him. And some of us would start do so, and he would then gasp at our superior understanding and make us believe that we were clever and wise. He would flatter us thus, and then he would take up his exciting narrative where he had left off and we would know that he was quicker and more cunning than we could ever be.

He would sometimes look at the women and mutter seductive words to them and it would make the men fidgety and Mabrooka would have to be restrained. But he was too crafty ever to go too far in that uneasy direction and he would then rapidly turn the whole thing into a farce by pretending to break wind loudly in the middle of a tender declaration of undying love. The eruption of bawdy

laughter that followed was, on one memorable occasion —
as I was later informed by Mahroos — the subject of a
threatening complaint to Abu Bakr from the Pasha's wife
via the Nubian gardener, who, as it happened had attended
as a guest and had laughed himself to a near seizure.

And so the stories went on and they bred other stories
which reshaped themselves endlessly in my head and
continued to do so when I grew into a man. Looking back
over the years, I realize that the old Travelling Teller of
Tales was using all the traditional dramatic manipulative
devices and tricks of the theatre and the movies and of
many great actors, devices that I have recognized time and
again, recurring almost like a dejà vu. . . because that
cunning old Arab had done it all before. But how did he
discover those techniques? Were they things he had learned
for himself by observation? Perhaps it came about through
a special intuitive understanding of his fellow humans? Or
by watching the reactions of his audience? Perhaps the
stories themselves led to such inventions through constant
repetition? Or did his talent grow out of necessity, just as
some actors will invent something new for every
performance to avoid going crazy with boredom and losing
track of the meaning of words. And perhaps it was all of
these things. Or none?

There is one thing more I had almost forgotten to mention. . .
another remarkable device of his. He did not invent it,
but he practised it with great skill. He would sometimes
tell a story on two levels at the same time. One level was
for the benefit of the children in the audience and the
other, usually erotic, was for the adults. He achieved this
by the use of words that had a double meaning, and with
ambiguous gestures that were interpreted in their different
ways by children and by adults. . . although this was not
always the case because we children, like children

everywhere, kept our ears open and our mouths shut when grown-ups talked about certain things in guarded terms, and we soon thought we had it figured out — sometimes with a little help from the older siblings.

There was, for instance, the tale of Ali Baba and the forty thieves. . . or fifty thieves with our story teller, perhaps because the word *khamseen*, meaning fifty in Arabic, is also the word for a sirocco, the hot desert wind that creates sandstorms, and that pun would have enabled him to weave an allegorical thread into his narrative. Yes, it was the double meanings of certain key words that he used cunningly in order to tell two separate stories and make them appear as one. When, for instance, the hero speaks the magic words: *'Iftaahe ya simsim'*, which mean *'Open sesame'* in Arabic, and the cave entrance opens to give him access to its hidden treasure, the knowing and appreciative adults in the audience were aware that the word *'simsim'* also refers to that other most desirable feminine gateway to a very different treasure in the arcane vocabulary of eroticism. Europeans could not be expected to be privy to those ambiguities and so they continue through the ages to enjoy, and to tell their own children these delightful Eastern fables on the same artless level as we children were intended to hear them from the Teller of Tales.

And finally, when the very young children could no longer stay awake, and the older children, in a twilit state between febrile wakefulness and unconquerable sleepiness, would be sent to their beds, the Teller of Tales would squat down on his haunches, warm his hands before the glowing embers of the charcoal brazier that would be brought to brew the tea on, and, without any histrionics, would get down to the serious business of conversing with the older members of that tightly bound but free spirited family community and bringing them up to date with the latest news about events in the outside world, which, as far as they were concerned, may not have been much more distant than the nearest village a few kilometres away. But by that time, I would be fast asleep in Mabrooka's lap.

There were other itinerant story tellers, lean and weary men, dusty from travel, who would squat down without ceremony and tell a few stories, often absently as though their thoughts were distanced from the over-familiar yarns they were reciting by rote. Their audiences were always sparse, consisting mainly of children who would soon get bored and start chattering or run off and play. I would feel shame and misery for those sad men, and I would try to make up for all the indifference by applauding wildly at the end of each banal tale delivered with laboured monotony. I still have that compulsion to do the same because I cannot bear to witness the flop of a performance — what is known in show business as 'dying the death'. But this story has quite a happy ending, because thirty one years later Hassan, a grandson of Abu Bakr, informed me that our Teller of Tales had expired long ago, while in mid-performance.

When the time comes, I should very much like to expire in the same way.

The Donkey

My name, by the way, is Edward Denys Garnett. I am
retired now because my employers have decided, in their
infinite wisdom, that I should make way for a younger man.
I was pleased for the young man, of course, and grateful
for the generous pension and the gold wristwatch — but
what was I to do with all the empty time that had been
thrust into my life? Perhaps I should start telling a few tall
tales of my own.

The Bedouin children and I greatly enjoyed the stories
about Goha told by the Travelling Teller of Tales. And so
did the grown-ups, not so much because they were simple
people who were easily amused, but because adults from
every culture throughout the ages have always relished
bawdy tales: the piquant seduction of haughty virtuous
ladies; the ingenious plucking of rich men's closely
guarded skittish daughters' maidenheads; the outrageous
cuckoldings of arrogant husbands in their own beds by their
lustful wives; the uninhibited ribaldry of scatological
vignettes and carnal escapades. These have always drawn
laughter from all but the most prudish, squeamish, or
genuinely shockable persons.

We may not understand the nature of laughter, but we know
what makes us laugh, and it's more often than not
something salacious. After all, religious chronicles, no less
than Far Eastern and Arabian fables, or Greek and Indian
and Polynesian legends, or Viking epics, or Chaucerian and

Rabelaisian tales, and, in all likelihood, the whole history
of humankind from the beginning of consciousness, are all
spiced with hilarious sexual mischief. But, in fairness, I
would not expect the Pope and the Holy See to see things
in quite the same light. I have my reasons for saying that.

All humour contains an element of cruelty, and for every
victor in a joke, there has to be a victim to some degree or
other. We have to identify with the victor in order to laugh.
The jokes in which we must grieve for the victim are never
funny. . . and they do not belong in the bright precincts of
humour, but in the murky mansions of injured spirits. Yet
some stories can contain a joke that makes us laugh as well
as a tragedy that can draw our tears, and sometimes, when
we are not quite sure whether to laugh or cry, we can do
both.

My first choice is a short and simple story and I would be
surprised and at the same time delighted if it made anyone
laugh, because, after all, it is not being told right now by
the old Teller of Tales stomping about and raising the dust
around him in the light of the paraffin lamps. Or is it?

             *   *   *

One fine day, our friend Goha is riding to the town on his
donkey as usual. But what's up? His eyes are filled with
tears. He's looking put out, melancholy, sad. . . one might
even go so far as to say that he is grief-stricken. Goha?
Grief-stricken? Has his wife passed away? Or worse,
thrown him out again and refused to prepare his only meal
of the day during Ramadan? No no, it's not because he is
hungry, indeed, he has had a fine meal of lentils flavoured
with olives and sliced onion with a ripe tomato and pickled
green chili, and his palate has been sweetened with crisp

red dates and a watermelon borrowed from the King's estate and which Goha intends to return discreetly at the earliest opportunity, albeit as fertilizer. No, the truth of the matter is that Goha's donkey is now too old to work and Goha cannot bear the thought of pushing the faithful animal into the canal. Besides, the obstinate beast would probably swim over to the other side and bray reproachfully at Goha who would then have to swim across to retrieve the wretched creature, probably catch a fatal chill, and depart from this life before the old donkey does.

Oh Almighty One, cast thy merciful gaze upon this thy faithful near-pilgrim Goha, who would have made it to Mecca had he not been assaulted by Yemeni bandits who claimed he had swindled them. Alas, how could he have known that the Holy Prophet's dagger he had sold to them, that priceless relic exquisitely engraved with cabalistic inscriptions, had been made in a mysterious country called Japan that he never knew even existed? What a terrible injustice!

And Goha's patience and his loyalty to his donkey are being tested almost beyond endurance. . . our poor friend who has, in a life already so full of hardships, suffered greater travails than the King's chief eunuch — with a couple of palpable exceptions, needless to say — is in a most distressing quandary. But enough of this, enough! Otherwise our compassionate fellow-feeling will become too unbearable to allow us to continue with this tale.

Now at this very moment, the donkey, having earlier devoured a large quantity of clover in Abdel Moossa's field into which Goha had inadvertently allowed him to stray while he, Goha, rested under the shade of the aromatic fig tree. . . at this very moment, I declare, within sight of the town market, the donkey has released a volley of zaraats that would have done justice to the cannonades discharged on every anniversary of His Majesty the King's ascendancy to the throne. Thanks to Allah that it had not taken place anywhere near an open flame, otherwise the highly combustible gases emitted from the donkey's rear would have ignited and caused a serious conflagration in which both the donkey and Goha would have been consumed on the spot. On the other hand of course, it would have resolved the whole problem once and for all.

But wait! Our Goha is, as we have come to expect, struck by an inspired notion. He decides to call on the wealthy merchant Mustapha Abu Labban, whose house is only a short distance away. He knocks on the door, and it is opened by Abu Labban's senior wife who welcomes Goha into the courtyard while explaining that the Master of the house is at the tea-house in the marketplace.

It seems that the worthy woman is most concerned about the distressing condition of one of their beautiful young daughters . . . a mysterious condition that causes the wretched girl to itch in the most intimate regions during the day and to moan and sigh pitifully during the night. Knowing that Goha is wise in matters of science and medicine (his having travelled widely and almost reached Mecca) she wonders if he can perform a remedy. He assures the mother that he can indeed, and most willingly. But he must be left alone with the young woman because his esoteric treatment is one to which he has been sworn to secrecy by the practitioners of the sacred art. The daughter, not surprisingly in view of Goha's unusual skills, responds most favourably to his gratifying therapy, which she found most pleasurable, and expresses the need for regular house calls from our caring healer.

Goha cunningly secretes the silver coins he has received in payment for his service and in pursuance of his fiendishly clever plan to dispose of the donkey makes his way to the tea-house to pay his respects to the girl's father, Abu Labban.

The corpulent merchant is seated in the company of his wealthy companions, with whom he has been gleefully exchanging anecdotes about profitable transactions in which some poor wretch or other has been reduced to penury. He is drawing smoke contentedly from the amber mouthpiece of the freshly prepared hubble-bubble at his side as Goha bows his head and addresses his jovial social superiors:

"Salaam upon you, effendis. I beg you to excuse my haste, but I must hurry to barter my old donkey for a fine young camel from the Moroccan nomad dealer". As he bows again and is about to leave, Goha prods the donkey firmly in the belly and is rewarded with a windy detonation. This discharges a silver coin that he furtively retrieves from the ground and places nonchalantly in his waistcoat pocket. He then raises his fist and curses the incontinent animal for its lack of decorum in the presence of such respectable gentlemen.

Abu Labban, with a condescending grin, remarks to Goha: "Is this worthy donkey expressing its opinion of your wisdom from the appropriate orifice, Goha, or is it merely protesting at your highly original choice of repository for a money bag?"

Goha, looking mortified, replies: "No no, Ya Bey, my moneybag is in my belt under my ghallabeya, here, kindly observe. But it is of no consequence, even though that foolish flatulent donkey has betrayed my little secret. Forgive me, but I must be on my way"

"Wait, wait!" cries out the merchant, his eyes narrowing greedily "What. . . erhhh. . . what little secret?"

"Oh, it was only a minor spell cast on my donkey by a travel weary Nubian sorcerer in gratitude for my offering him a ride on the beast. A trifling thing, upon my faith, but since you ask, I am honour bound to disclose to you the source of my recent good fortune. You see, noble sir, every time the donkey breaks wind, he also magically discharges a silver coin. I am about to exchange him for a camel which clearly has a more generous capacity. But see for yourself, Ya Bey: kindly oblige me by prodding the beast. . . yes, I pray you, right there"

The merchant does so three times, and each time the gaseous blast from the animal is followed by a silver coin.

Abu Labban's rapacious nature now fully aroused, he is almost beside himself with greed. But being a man skilled in the art of adroit haggling he maintains an outward demeanour of benign indifference as he wags a finger at the donkey: "I am a generous man, Goha, reputed for fair dealing, am I not? Have I not often been mocked behind my back for paying too high a price for short-weight sacks of grain and for short-length bolts of cloth? Admit it! Yes, it is my charitable nature for which my wives are constantly chiding me, is this not the case? Women, alas, do not understand these things. I'll tell you what I am prepared to do, Goha my dear honest fellow, I am willing to take that decrepit animal off your hands for. . . listen, I am about to make an absurdly over-generous offer. . . for, say, fifty Rials and may the good Prophet gaze kindly upon you"

"I am overwhelmed, Ya Bey, by your kindness, which knows no bounds, but I cannot take advantage of you by accepting. . . no no, it is impossible. Supposing the spell wears off? No no, it is out of the question. . ."

"Observe, I am a benefactor of humankind. . . one hundred Rials, cash down!"

"But if the worse should happen — Allah forbid — these spells carry no warranty. . . it would prey upon my conscience. . ."

"The devil with your wretched conscience! No, no, what I mean is, don't worry dear faithful Goha. Should the spell be broken, well, you can take that revolting animal and shove it up. . . I mean dump it in the. . . no, let us be reasonable. . . one hundred and fifty Rials and that's the limit!"

"You drive such a hard bargain, Ya Bey, that you must surely be guided by the hand of the Spirit of Powerful Merchants. I realize that it would be an affront to that Spirit if I were now to disobey your command. Two hundred Rials, did you say?"

And so they shook hands on the bargain. The merchant paid up and, anxious to test his new acquisition in the presence of his friends, hurriedly bade Goha call at his house on his way back and tell the women, on the master's instructions, that they were to provide his good friend Goha with a generous helping of the sweetmeats freshly prepared for the banquet in celebration of the end of Ramadan. Our friend left eagerly, for he had earlier sampled a delectable sweetmeat at the merchant's home and it had been much to his taste. That merchant's generosity indeed knew no bounds, even though the poor fool was not fully aware of the true extent of his magnanimity.

Back at the tea-house, Abu Labban has lifted the donkey's tail and positioned himself in such a manner as to observe at very close quarters the emergence of a quick profit from his investment. Far be it for me to try your patience and to offend your sensibilities with a detailed description of what followed after Abu Labban gave the animal a powerful jab in the stomach. . . I daresay you may be well aware that a feast of fresh clover fermenting into a ferociously noisome brew in the innards of an ass must of necessity find the appropriate outlet from which to discharge itself if the inflated creature is not to fly into a thousand fragments. My wise and honourable friends, this is a proven and incontrovertible scientific fact which had been recorded in the learned books of our Great Library of Alexandria.

And thus we have reached the tail end of this story, as it were, with a chastened and perhaps slightly wiser merchant Abu Labban; with the donkey, much relieved of its discomfort and finding its own way back to the field of clover and with our friend Goha in a much happier frame of mind. Ah yes, for it's an ill wind. . .

The Nuns

It was a hot and humid day in August when I was taken by my father to visit Madame Kyriakides. After a short while she left the room and we were left sitting on our own at the table in front of the balcony. I noticed that my father's hands were shaking slightly as he removed his pince-nez and cleaned the lenses with the white handkerchief that he kept neatly folded in the front pocket of his jacket. After he had replaced the handkerchief he made sure that the bit protruding above the pocket formed an accurate isosceles triangle. Of course, I did not know what an isosceles triangle was at the time, but later, when I went to school, I was able to recognize the shape instantly.

My father seemed upset about something because his eyes were filled with tears. When he blinked the tears rolled quickly over his lower lids like small crystal beads and fell onto his lapels where they disappeared into the linen fabric leaving dark oval stains. He spoke quietly in French because I could only speak that language, apart from Bedouin Arabic, which my father did not understand.

"Listen, my son, your mother, you know, is not well. She's quite ill with her nerves in fact, and all that worrying about you constantly makes her worse. Do you understand? So you are going to stay with Madame Kyriakides for a while and she will look after you very well I'm sure. Moreover, her daughter Helen will teach you things from books, very interesting things, you'll see. Your mother is most upset

that you spend so much time with those Bedouin
children. . . they are uneducated little savages and you are
beginning to grow like them and that's no good really, is it
now? Helen will teach you things that will be very useful
to you when you go to school so your mother will not be
ashamed of you. . . no no, what I mean is: so that we'll be
proud of you, you understand?"

"Will I go to school with the Pasha's daughters in the
King's car, to where there are mountains and snow?"

"What King's car? The King's cars are crimson and black.
Where did you see the King's car? Do please be sensible
now. That's just the kind of thing that troubles your
mother. . . when you make up stories like that. Anyway,
you must behave yourself with Madame Kyriakides, and if
you don't I'm afraid she will tell your mother and you
won't be able to come home for a very long time because
she will be too upset with you. Now there's one more thing:
you won't be able to see Grandmama again because she's
very ill and we may have to look after her before she goes
to heaven, you see, so she will have to have your room for
some time"

"Did I make Grandmama ill? Please Papa, she could stay
with Mabrooka. Why can't she stay with Mabrooka? . .
Mabrooka will look after her, then I can come home, can't
I?"

"How could you possibly make Grandmama ill, my son?
No no of course you didn't. . . what could have put such
an idea into your little head? No, it's not as simple as that.
Anyway, Grandmama can't go and live with these people.
Mabrooka, my God, she is a most unsuitable person. . . I
mean Grandmama wouldn't like it at all. Can't you
understand that? She couldn't possibly. . . it would be quite
out of the question. I wonder what makes you say things
like that? You see, that's precisely the strange kind of thing

you say that causes your dear mother so much anxiety.
Anyway, we have decided that you must not see those
children from Abu Bakr any more. We have told Madame
Kyriakides so, and she will not allow you out on your own.
Those horrendous stories from the Bedouins you told
Grandmama. . . she was quite shocked. . . she had never
heard anything like it. She blamed your poor mother, which
was most upsetting for me. It's all very puzzling. And I'm
afraid that your ghallabeya had to be thrown away. . . yes
my little one, I know how fond of it you must have been.
But you must now wear proper clothes as well as your
sandals all the time. In any case, you are almost seven years
old and must be taught to live like a civilised person from
now on. And, above all, you must be obedient and always
on your best behaviour with Madame. It was very kind of
her to take you in at short notice. Yes, well, I must go
now, my boy. I shall try and come round to see you soon. . .
one day, soon. . . so au revoir, au revoir dear son. Oh, I
have given Madame some money to get you an ice cream
from time to time. I know how much you like pistachio ice
cream"

The ice cream rarely materialized and I was not to see my
mother again for several months, although my father visited
me about once every two weeks and paid Madame
Kyriakides the money for my upkeep.

I did not see my grandmother again, but I discovered many
years later that she had left a gold brooch to my mother in
her will and nothing at all to me. I was not too disappointed
though, because I had not expected to be given anything
when she died — other than the big grandfather clock with
the long swinging pendulum and musical chimes, the
echoing notes of which I was to remember all my life. I
would have liked to have inherited the polished brass
dinner gong and the small alabaster elephant too, but I

would happily have settled for the grandfather clock on its
own. Maybe Grandmama had taken it to heaven with her.

Of course I was too young to have been told about Last
Wills and Testaments and it would not have mattered much
if I had. What did matter was that I had lost my
Grandmama and that I had given some serious thought as
to where and to what heaven might be. I had not come to
any meaningful conclusion about that but had decided
instead that I would undoubtedly find out when I went to
heaven. I would tell Grandmama that I was sorry about the
rude stories and then she might give me the grandfather
clock.

I did not cry when my father left, but there was a heaviness
in my head, as though it had a large stone in it, a sensation
I was to feel many times again throughout my life when
things were bad. It is hard now to fathom my feelings in
any depth because they were all swirling in the depths of a
child's unique version of reality. But I do know that my
mind would still be clinging to the things that were now
suddenly lost to me. That way they might remain accessible
for a little while longer until they were returned to me, or
until I could come to terms with their permanent absence.
Some little animals, when they are filled with fear, fall into
a deep sleep, and I must have done just that, because when
Madame Kyriakides came into the room after my father had
left, she found me curled up under the dining table. She
would no doubt have concluded that my contact with the
Bedouins had indeed turned me into a 'petit sauvage' — as
I was referred to in that household from that day on, not
always without some affection it must be said.

Madame Kyriakides lived with her son Kyriako and her
daughter Helen in a small flat above the grocer's shop
across the road from the convent. There was a small narrow
balcony leading off the dining room, and that balcony was

to become my only perspective view from which I would daily observe a minute section of the world carrying out its regular routine. It was therefore the tiniest variations in that routine that I watched out for: a stranger walking down the road; an unfamiliar car driving up to the convent, carrying men wearing long black cloaks and funny hats; a young new nun ordering the girls to keep silent as they walked across the playground; different produce being delivered to the shop below as the crop seasons changed — and enormous round cheeses with a mouth-watering aroma that I could smell from my vantage point above and the resinous perfume of the pinewood planks arriving at the carpenter's shop next door; a familiar stray dog limping with its tail between its legs, when it was running around foraging for rotting tidbits the day before; the flapping of migrating quail flying low overhead; a cat running furtively across the road with one of its kittens dangling from its mouth; a pair of hoopoe in the large ficus tree in the convent yard. There was an abundance of interesting details to note.

For months on end I spent all my days on that balcony, only leaving it at meal-times or to go to the bathroom, or sometimes, to go for a walk with Kyriako on a Sunday afternoon.

At first, my little friends from Abu Bakr would come round every day to call out to me to come down and play with them. But they soon tired of doing that when they realized I was unable to join them. Besides, they were always chased away by the grocer's assistant, which would have been fun for the first few times, and not so much fun later when he took to throwing stones at them. I was relieved when they stopped coming because their calls were a painful reminder of one of the most treasured things I had lost.

Some distance down the road on my right I could see just
a few feet of the bottom of the garden where my parents
lived. Several times I had seen Mahroos rummaging in the
bushes, probably for one of the rabbits that may have
escaped from its cage, but my hope of catching a glimpse
of my mother was not fulfilled even though I would
instinctively peer in that direction throughout the day.
Eventually it became a reflexive action unaccompanied by
any real expectation of seeing her figure in the distance.
But I could still see her face very clearly in my mind's eye
and it would have given me great comfort to have been able
to wave to her so that she would know that she was not
forgotten.

The nuns often waved discreetly to me, and they must have
wondered what that little boy was doing up on that balcony,
like a sailor lad in a crow's nest looking out to sea,
constantly searching for sight of land and shading his eyes
with his hand against the bright sunlight.

One day an elderly nun appeared at the door and Madame
Kyriakides agreed to her request for me to be allowed to
visit the convent. She explained, as we walked across the
road that no man was ever allowed on the holy premises,
apart from priests, who weren't ordinary men but servants
of God. I wondered if they did strange things like the
Nubian gardener. He was a servant too.

The fuss the girls made over me! Several times the nuns
had to quieten them down as they jostled one another to
hold my hand as I was escorted round the convent. A couple
of the girls boldly kissed me on the cheek while the
supervising nun was pretending to look away. An elderly
fat rosy-cheeked nun in the kitchen actually picked me up
and hugged me so hard that it squeezed the breath out of
me. And when she had put me down she turned away
suddenly and I noticed that she was wiping her eyes with

her apron. Later I joined them in the dining hall, and after Mother Superior had said Grace, they feasted me with enormous helpings of food.

After the meal the girls loaded me with sweets and bars of chocolate that they had retrieved from their dormitory lockers. I have remembered that day all my life and, some years later, when I was studying for the priesthood, there was one thing that I treasured above all my meagre possessions: it was the crucifix that the nun from the kitchen had stuffed into my pocket as I was leaving the convent. And a few years after that, some time after I had stopped believing in the existence of a God, it would be this precious object that I would always carry with me at a time when I had been thrust into a war about which I and my comrades understood so little. No, I had not intended to mention that in this story. It seemed inappropriate. But on second thoughts it may not be so because, you see, I still remember that old nun as clearly as though she were standing right here beside me, about to crush the breath out of me.

And why do I remember Helen Kyriakides so vividly? Well, I'm about to tell you.

The flat consisted of a tiny entrance lobby where Kyriako's rarely used raincoat and umbrella hung on a rack behind the door; then a dining and living room with a narrow corridor on the left leading to a small kitchen opposite a bathroom, and, at the end of the corridor, two bedrooms. And there was the balcony off the dining room.

Helen shared one bedroom with her mother and I slept on a folding bed in Kyriako's room. He hardly ever spoke to me other than to say 'no'. It was a word into which he had introduced an endless variety of self-expressive meaning and subtle nuances. These ranged from direct prohibition through sarcastic incredulity to a few rare positive thoughts and philosophical musings, generally with regard to the perverseness of his fellow-humans. Sometimes he would simply say 'no' as a bland signal that he was about to go to the lavatory or have a bath or go for a walk.

He would occasionally shake his head sadly and say 'no' in a tone of voice that I would take as an affirmative response to my request to accompany him on his stroll to the sea shore. On those walks he would point at the colourful approaching sunset and use that word in a way that clearly indicated he was refuting some absent person's argument that the sunset was not the miraculous phenomenon that Kyriako believed it to be. He sometimes said 'no' sharply in his sleep, which would make my heart leap with sudden guilt, until I got used to it and learned to respond with a firm 'no!' of my own. This seemed to reassure and quieten him in whatever uneasy dream he was resentfully participating at that precise moment.

He would have been in his early twenties at the time. Quite short and very thin, in spite of the enormous quantity of food his mother prepared for him and which he ate very quickly, often with his left arm placed protectively round his plate as though preventing an unseen predator from snatching it away from him.

On alternate days she would bring to the boil and simmer a litre of milk that she would then pour into a large dish and store overnight in the ice-box. The following morning she would carefully roll off the thick skin of cream that had formed on the surface and place half of it in front of Kyriako for breakfast, saving the other half for the next day. He would cover it with strawberry jam and eat it with a fork and spoon. I would watch him doing this every morning eagerly hoping that he would let me have a taste of that great delicacy that made him look up at the ceiling and murmur an ecstatic 'no'. I only got to taste it once, and

I shall remember to describe the occasion — at the appropriate moment if you'll please bear with me. Previously, my only consolation was to receive a knowing smile and a wink from that otherwise morose individual as he slowly rolled his tongue round the pink confection.

Every morning Kyriako would spring from his bed with his hand firmly placed over the region where I knew that men were endowed with something that girls didn't have, and it was only several months later that I observed, after he had absentmindedly forgotten his ritual cover, that the front of his pyjama pants protruded several inches to form a kind of horizontal tent. I often wondered after that if the concealed object was identical to the one belonging to the Nubian gardener. He, at least, had shown some pride in his curious masculine condition. I had long known the purpose of the object in that solid state, although I was not quite sure what all the fuss and secrecy was about. But I nevertheless set out to discover, as cautiously as possible because I was undoubtedly venturing into hazardous adult territory, a little more about it than I had already gleaned from my Bedouin playmates whose knowledge was restricted to the graphic but hardly enlightening motion of forming a ring with two fingers of one hand and pumping a finger from the other hand into it and shrieking with laughter.

Madame Kyriakides was ruled out as a prospective source of information because of the unlikelihood of her ever having performed that mysterious act. There was, after all, no Monsieur Kyriakides, so that was that. Her two children, I concluded must have been produced by some other method. Especially Kyriako, who was weird and who had probably never been a baby, but had materialized just as he was now, with a scowl on his face and his jet black pomaded hairline barely an inch and a half above thick eyebrows that formed a straight unbroken dark stroke above his large expressionless eyes. His response to my enquiry would, I concluded, have been laconic to say the least. And nuns were definitely out, in spite of the Princess's postcards. So that left Helen as my potential informant.

Helen was probably about eighteen years old. I never discovered what she did after she left the house every morning. She returned in the afternoon at exactly the same time every day and took a hot bath before dinner. She played the upright piano in the dining room on week-ends and her favourite piece was Für Elise which she occasionally syncopated because it would irritate Kyriako who would bellow *'NO!'* from his bedroom or from the bathroom in which he spent a good deal of his time.

I would sometimes sit beside her and she would stretch my fingers over the keys and show me how to play chords. When she touched me I would feel a slight tingle like a barely perceptible electric shock and I would then have an irresistible urge to run my fingers very lightly all over her body and discover if I would experience the same little shocks, or maybe more powerful ones from other parts of her. It was very tantalizing, but I knew, somehow, that this might displease her, and that wouldn't do at all because she was my friend. And besides, if I was going to live there for very much longer, perhaps we could have a baby together when I was a bit older and then she wouldn't mind and it would be all right. And I wouldn't have to share a room with Kyriako because his mother would move in with him. I could move in with Helen, which would be so much more pleasant. I gave it much thought as I sat on the balcony.

Her hair was much lighter in colour than Kyriako's and she had an oval shaped face rather than the square one with high prominent cheekbones that he had inherited from his mother. One day, soon after I decided to pursue my quest

for greater discovery, and we were alone in the flat, I took
the next important step of examining Helen *'au naturel'*, by
looking through the keyhole while she was in the bathroom.

The sight I beheld was fascinating and entirely satisfactory:
her boyishly slender unblemished body was breathtakingly
symmetrical, including the two perfect hemispheres on her
chest. The triangle of black hair lower down was clear
evidence of her maidenly modesty. It was delightful and
totally rivetting — so much so, that I had overlooked the
fact that the bathroom door was glazed with frosted glass
and that she could see the outline of my little figure
crouched on the other side. She moved very quickly,
because I was suddenly confronted by that dewy triangle
only a few inches away from my flushed face after she had
swung open the door.

"Well little savage, are you satisfied now?" she asked with
a scolding smile. Her body was wet as, still crouching on
one knee, I boldly touched her kneecap and was rewarded
with a tiny spark.

"How did you do that?" she asked with amazement as she
stepped back. Encouraged by what I took to be her inviting
response, I stood up and followed her into the bathroom
which smelt of aromatic salts.

"Close the door. . ." she ordered quietly, sitting on the edge
of the bath "Now it's your turn. Take off your clothes and
we'll get you clean and smelling sweet"

I obeyed her and climbed into the bath. She then swung her
legs over gracefully and sat opposite me in the hot scented
soapy water. Next, she lifted me up gently and sat me
astride her legs and started to wash me all over, taking
particular care to be gentle with parts of me that might be
painful if handled roughly. I had never experienced
anything so deliciously comforting as the touch of her

fingers running arpeggios over my body. As she slid down
the bath in order to rinse off the soap, followed by my own
body on top of hers, I could feel her wiry mound of hairs
against my tingling tenderness. I timidly stroked her supple
hemispheres to test them for sparks, and there were none.
But Helen placed her hand on mine as I was about to
remove it, signalling that she wished me to continue. I did
not try to understand why that gave us both so much
pleasure.

We lay there for a long time, caressing each other and
occasionally brushing our lips and noses together lightly. It
seemed to me that there were small sparks exchanged when
we did that, and it made us both giggle. Suddenly we heard
the front door open and slam shut. Helen leapt up, rolling
me off and creating a tidal wave that slopped half the bath
water over the side. 'Bon Dieu' she whispered as she put
her hand over my mouth to quell my noisy spluttering. She
dried herself hurriedly and was slipping into her silk
bathrobe as Kyriako's dark silhouette walked past the door.

Our spontaneous encounter was never referred to, never
even hinted at, but she did teach me how to jazz up Für
Elise on the piano, and I would feel a thrill of joy at the
sight of her hands gliding over the keyboard.

Now and then, when she was sure that we were alone, she
would run her soft fingertips down my cheek and hold my
chin as though to steady my face as she bent down and
touched my lips briefly with hers. It would unfailingly
produce the minute spark that I took to be a confirmation
of our secret bond.

I would later recall the only words Helen had spoken while
we were sharing that joyful companionship in the bath. She
had held my head in her hands as she murmured: "Listen
my little savage, no man will ever be allowed to do this
with me".

The Novice

Kyriako Kyriakides had, one rainy Sunday morning, unexpectedly agreed to take me to Roman Catholic Mass. His casual 'no' to my request had sounded unconvincingly negative. It was a clear signal of reluctant consent, and so the black velvet short trousers, black patent leather shoes and white silk blouse were brought out of mothballs for that important occasion before the frowning young man could change his mind.

Even the Teller of Tales, in all his most colourful descriptions of exotic happenings, could not have prepared me for such an extraordinary experience: the priest's sacramental ritual at the altar; the incantations dramatically intoned in Latin; the deep murmured responses of the congregation contrasting with the tinkling of the sacring bell; the choir's descant voices in the missa cantata; the echoing acoustics in that high domed place of worship; the heady fumes of smouldering frankincense and sweet cicely bark that reminded me of the aroma of spices and crushed amber that Abu Bakr sprinkled on the charcoal embers of his incense burner. And most impressive of all was the priest's magnificently embroidered chasuble — such a vestment as could not possibly have existed outside the realm of fairy tales.

Entranced by all I had seen and heard, I informed Kyriako that I had definitely decided to become a priest and asked him how one would go about achieving that exciting and most desirable objective without delay. Kyriako, with his marked lack of enthusiasm for anything that failed to meet his standards for economy and restraint in all things, replied with great seriousness that the matter should be given prolonged and careful thought before taking any precipitate action that might later be regretted.

Undaunted by Kyriako's non-committal attitude, I then sought my father's guidance at the fortnightly visit a few days later. The solemn response that her son joining the priesthood would undoubtedly give my mother a *crise de nerfs* was disappointing although not entirely unexpected. But even that painful warning did little to alter my resolve that one day, in the not too distant future, I too would be conducting a mystical service before a worshipping congregation; enjoying the privilege of communing directly with an understanding God concealed behind the altar, and, above all, of wearing a beautifully embroidered golden ecclesiastical cloak that would delight my mother and father and impress Abu Bakr, Mahroos, Helen, Countess Zinnia, and, of course, the nuns — yes, most assuredly, the nuns. It would be very satisfying.

Some years later, while preparing for the priesthood, it gradually dawned on me that my true beliefs were leading me in a contrary direction. The whole idea of becoming a servant of God turned out to be impracticable, if not preposterous. It was out of the question, and the vanished prospect of wearing those exquisite pontifical vestments was a sacrifice I would therefore have to accept — it was the price I would have to pay for my total inability to commune with any kind of Superior Being whatsoever, or to accept or dispense any promises to my fellow-humans about the glories of everlasting life in a hereafter which I was confident could not possibly exist. It was both a relief and a disappointment.

The Princesses

The day finally arrived for me to return home. When I was about to say goodbye to Madame Kyriakides — my final farewell as it happens, for I was never to see her again after that day — she sat me at the dining room table and placed a dish of cream and a saucer of strawberry jam before me and left the room. She looked much paler than usual and appeared to have some problem with her mascara. I sat quietly, unsure of what I was supposed to do with the tantalizing delicacy that had been the object of my yearning for so long. Kyriako sat opposite me for a long time holding a spoon that he examined with all the concentration of an archaeologist examining a newly unearthed artifact. He handed it to me with an unfamiliar smile and gestured magnanimously toward the longed-for dessert. The overpowering flavour of that first mouthful was almost unbearable — I was experiencing for the first time the pain that sometimes accompanies a certain kind of pleasure. It had a quality that I instantly recognized on the rare occasions I experienced it throughout my life. I was to discover, too, that love can cause pain with a curiously similar flavour.

Yes I remember it clearly, I was licking the spoon clean when my father arrived to take me home. As we were about to leave, Madame Kyriakides held my face tightly for a few moments in her bony blue-veined hands and they felt surprisingly soft. Her mascara, I noticed, had become rather messy. Kyriako reached down to shake my hand briefly as he whispered 'no' in my ear. I had never heard that sad and wistful 'no' before. I replied with the same firm 'no' with which I had redirected his bad dreams in the past. He turned and walked onto my balcony and I could only see his back. Backs, I found out then, can convey their own silent messages.

But Helen was absent. She had not returned from whatever place she visited every week day. Would she, I wondered, have sat at the piano and bade me farewell with a mournful rendition of Für Elise? No, it was better this way.

My father and I did not go straight home. "Your mother is tired, she is having a rest right now" he explained, "she will see you before you go to bed. . . in the meanwhile we shall pay a visit to the Countess Zinnia"

Countesses, I concluded some years later, are not unlike an ubiquitous species of hardy shrub: they are fairly prolific, usually colourful, often exotically scented and invariably sensitive to the most minor changes in the social atmosphere. Zinnia was no exception.

The double doors of her boudoir slid apart as she glided toward us with her head thrown back slightly and her right hand outstretched at just the right height for me to brush it respectfully with my lips. She greeted us wearing a flowing diaphanous floral patterned house robe in pastel colours which blew around her in the airless drawing room as she moved, like the extravagantly billowing filmy sails of a hopelessly unseaworthy boat in an illustrated fairy tale.

It was, however, her two daughters and their friend by whom I was instantly charmed — I would have used the word 'seduced', but that is a word which has now been traduced so that it no longer means 'to charm'. I think that's a pity.

Sunneya and Noora were in their mid teens, as was their companion whom they called Safi. The three girls immediately took possession of me as though they had been presented with a living toy. They took me to their suite and after washing my face and hands and knees several times, quite unnecessarily I felt at the time, and combing my hair in a variety of comical styles that sent them into fits of giggles and which made me tighten my lips with surliness, they perfumed me and kissed me in turn all over my face and neck, which I also considered entirely uncalled for and, at the same time, strangely pleasant. They then asked my father's permission to take me to the open-air cinema at the San Stephano Casino on the sea-front.

I had never been to the cinema before, and as I sat beside Safi, deeply engrossed in the wondrous events taking place on the screen, with the moonlit sea in the background, she lifted the back of my silk blouse and was about to touch my back when a small spark suddenly bridged that tiny gap and she withdrew her hand with a barely perceptible intake of breath. But I had noticed it, and I was in love again.

The four of us were frequent companions after that, and Safi's affectionate attention and gentle teasing, coupled with my easy ability to make her laugh, convinced me with no room for doubt that she and I would make a baby together at the proper time and live happily ever after. I had, of course, felt some guilt toward Helen for depriving her of the future happiness that we would otherwise have shared, but I sensibly decided that the prospect of forfeiting a happy future with an even more beautiful woman would entail far too great a sacrifice on my part. Love can be so inconstant!

I was also to find out, some months later, just how cruel love can be when it conspires with fate to frustrate the

honourable and solemn aspirations of a very young human
male.

Farida — for that was her new name — had not joined us
as usual at the San Stephano Casino. She had, the girls told
me, been betrothed to King Farouk of Egypt. I had lost my
beloved Princess.

Some years later, after she had been divorced by her
beautiful but gross and impetuous king for failing to
provide him with a son and heir, I found the magazine
cutting I had kept of Farida's wedding photograph and felt
melancholy for the rest of the day, pondering absurdly over
the lingering and impossible fantasy of 'what might have
been'.

And many years later I learned of the death of that other
Princess, the one who had invited me for coffee and a
Turkish cigarette, and I created another quite different and
intriguing tale about what might have happened during her
last encounter with the lover who was the cause of her royal
disgrace and banishment to solitary luxury.

                    *   *   *

The handsome grey-haired man wearing a black mohair
pinstripe suit had removed his tarboosh, the traditional red
felt headgear that looked like an overturned flower pot with
a black silk tassel swinging over its side, and he had placed
it carefully on the small round table inlaid with
mother-of-pearl mosaic. He had then flicked a speck of dust
off the tassel before moving to the window.

That nervously casual gesture irritated the Princess. She
thought it was beneath his dignity to stoop to insignificant
gestures on this exceptionally important occasion, and even
though he may not have been aware of its importance, it

was, nonetheless, impertinent of him to adopt a nonchalant air in her presence. The fact that he was her lover and much older that herself should make no difference whatsoever: she was a Princess of the royal blood and he was merely an Assistant Chamberlain. She had, admittedly, allowed him to take certain liberties in the bed-chamber and to set aside for a short while the social chasm that divided them. . . but even in the intimate privacy that they had *enjoyed,* so to speak, there were certain immutable conventions that had to be observed. There was the ever present risk that too much familiarity on one's part would be taken advantage of by non-royal persons who would then get ideas above their station.

Had not her father Ismail. . . grandson of Mohammed Ali the Great. . . her beloved father whom she had hardly ever seen because he was otherwise occupied with affairs of state or attending to his concubines. . . had he not warned her of this danger when she was still young enough to sit on his royal knee? Had her brother Fuad not had the gardener in charge of the experimental hybrid melon plantation beaten because the wretched man had made an impertinent remark to her when she was a young girl? Oh yes, the palace courtiers could take liberties with her nephew Farouk, the future monarch, and get away with it because he relied on them to procure those European women for him. . . and he was only sixteen years old, the little fool. It was disgraceful, yes, and she knew why Fuad had done no more than lose his temper with his ministers from time to time and shout for hours on end until he had reduced everyone in the palace to tears of terror. But that was all he could do, yes, because they obtained the same women for him too. These women were without shame, often the wives of foreign diplomats. Perhaps they believed that being penetrated by the Royal Member during a

fleeting interregnum between sheets might advance their
husbands' careers. Or, more likely, so that they could boast
about it to their women friends. . . or even to their
husbands. Stupid creatures. And sometimes Fuad and
Farouk would get each others' castoffs. It was revolting. It
was hardly surprising that Farouk was having to undergo
treatment for that disgusting condition which, he had told
her, was like pissing scalding hot rose water, the obscene
little animal. Goodness only knows how widely the
abominable disease was being spread around. The foreign
embassies must be in a panic. . . all except the Turks and
the Albanians who were perverts anyway. He would
probably pass on the infection to some poor sweet girl he
would eventually marry, the vile pig. Oh, it didn't bear
thinking about. Certainly not right now.

The man was a dark silhouette as he stood with his back to
the open window. The strong sunlight had narrowed her
pupils to pinpoints and she looked lynx-like as she squinted
angrily at him, trying to make out the expression on his
shadowed face.

The wretched fellow was quite impossible, she decided. He
must have placed himself in that position in order to put
her at a disadvantage. Her brother Fuad always did that: he
would sit at his enormous desk with his back to the large
french windows so that people would be blinded by the
light and not be able to make out the expression on his face.
He would pull funny faces, horrid grimaces, and think that
they couldn't be seen. But they were, and some people
thought he had some awful tic, or that he was mad. Oh, her
brother was mad all right, no doubt about it. His bodyguard
had even had to have bullet-proof glass fitted in the window
in case some madman decided to shoot him in the back
while he was playing his silly games. And now this fool of
a lover was aping his master. It was most annoying and, in

any case, it was irresponsible because he could easily be seen by the servants in the courtyard and they would immediately report his presence in her chamber to the King. Well, she would deal with that later, but right now there was something much more important and urgent on her mind. She tried to sound nonchalant as she sat on the sofa. She fitted a black Balkan Sobranie cigarette into an ivory holder and lit it. Twisting her Cartier diamond bracelet casually round her wrist, she whispered through clenched teeth:

"You will have to kill Fuad"

He coughed with surprise and discreetly swallowed the phlegm before whispering hoarsely: "What did you say? Kill Fuad? Did you say kill him? Your brother? The King? His Majesty the King?"

"How many Fuads are there on the throne? Of course I meant His Majesty the King" she shouted, failing to suppress the bitter sarcasm in that reference to her brother's majestic title.

"But he's your brother, the King. You must be out of your mind. Oh God, how can I possibly kill him? Why? Why should I kill him? No no, I think I can guess why you have this insane idea in your head. But to kill His Majesty!"

"Shoot him"

"Shoot him? You mean with a bullet?"

"Yes shoot him. With a gun and with bullets. Would you shoot him with a cucumber you fool?"

"I am not a fool. Don't call me a fool. Of course you shoot someone with a gun. You don't shoot someone with a cucumber. That's obvious. What are you talking about? You are mad. The servants all say you are mad, and please stop shouting"

"The servants? What do the servants know? Have you been talking to the servants about me? You have been talking to the servants about me. Don't deny it. What have you been telling them? Why do you talk to the servants about me? How shameful of you. Have you no shame? No respect for me at all? Well, have you been talking to the servants about me? It's contemptible. Tell me at once, have you?"

"Of course not. How can you think such a thing! Allow me to remind you that I am an Assistant Chamberlain to His Majesty and I have a position to maintain. You see how unreasonable you are sometimes. You are always accusing me of doing bad things. It's quite intolerable"

"Oh really? What about that English woman last year?"

"English woman?"

"My God. . . are you going to pretend. . ."

"Oh, *that* one. I knew you were going to bring that up again. I explained it all to you at the time: she was just a friend, the British Consul's sister. We only went shooting jerboa on His Majesty's estate near Mex together, that's all. She was much too skinny for my taste and flat-chested and she smoked cigarettes at the breakfast table. I can't even remember her name. . . there, you see. Look, I have to be accommodating with these people otherwise that old fool the British Ambassador makes trouble for His Majesty. You know what he does, he wags his finger at His Majesty and reminds him that it was the British who put him on the throne in the first place and that they can just as easily remove. . ."

"Well, you'd better shoot him then"

"What? Shoot the British Ambassador? Excuse me, sweet one, but I don't quite follow. Besides, His Majesty wouldn't approve"

"No, why don't you listen. Obviously not the British Ambassador you fool, although I daresay that it wouldn't be such a bad idea. . . the man's a pig. . . did you see the way that he leered at me at the palace reception last month? Yes, His Majesty. . . His Majesty. . . that's all you can talk about, His absurd Majesty. But there's no need for you to be servile about him in my presence. I am perfectly well aware of your true opinion of him. That's not what you called him last night when you were enjoying my body. . . you were crying. . . you were telling me you would die for loving me. You hurt me. Look at your teeth marks on my. . ."

"Please, spare me your martyrdom and do not expose yourself in this manner. Do up your dress, please. It's most undignified. Anyway, you seemed to be enjoying the experience as I recall. I thought you liked a little pain. . ."

"A little pain! You almost bit it off, you animal. Now, are you going to shoot him?"

"I wish you wouldn't keep saying that. You are shouting and someone will hear you. You know what your servants are like"

"You promised. You made promises, remember. You have been telling me for the past eight years that you would ask Fuad for my hand in marriage after you divorced your other wives. I trusted you and you have lied to me"

"That is unfair and unreasonable if I may say so. I did in fact touch upon the subject to His Majesty in a roundabout way a year or two ago and he pretended not to hear what I was saying. That must surely have been his way of warning me that the subject should not be pursued, don't you agree? You did agree at the time, didn't you? And there was no talk then of shooting His Majesty, so why has this insane notion suddenly entered that beautiful head of yours. I have

to tell you that all this talk of disposing of His Majesty has
somehow aroused me. There, you see, I am confessing to a
little madness myself, madness for you my beautiful one. . .
an uncontrollable desire to take your body in my arms and
bite. . ."

"Wait, wait. And *then* will you shoot him?"

"We'll see. We'll see. Come now. . . I don't have much
time to spare. Have you locked the door my sweet?"

*   *   *

Now I should bring this apocryphal story to a swift end,
with its tragic consequences for two persons at least. But
there is a little more to tell before I do so. You see, that
last encounter between the Princess and her lover was
overheard by a chambermaid who described it to His
Majesty's Head Chef who divulged it to the Head
Chauffeur's wife who repeated it to her husband who
dutifully informed his Royal Master who immediately
ordered his Head of Palace Security to have both the
Assistant Chamberlain and the Head Chauffeur
'accidentally' shot dead the following night while the Royal
entourage were hunting gazelles by spotlight at the King's
desert lodge near Lake Mariout. No one, by the way, had
warned the unfortunate Head Chauffeur that, by some
ancient traditions, the bearer of bad news was almost
invariably executed unless he made himself scarce until the
whole nasty business blew over. That is very sad because
the poor man was only thirty-two years old when he
delivered his fateful message to his beloved monarch. His
Majesty was, let it be known, a strict observer of some of
the finest traditions of the ancient Parthians, from whom he
believed he was descended.

The Princess was understandably distraught when she received the news of her lover's death from the tearful chambermaid who had been indiscreet but who was, in fact, getting considerable pleasure from the incident in which she believed she had played a central role.

The Princess ran furiously all the way through the palace, along Axminster-carpeted crystal-chandeliered corridors — twice turning the wrong corner and straying, first into the Throne Room and then into the Byzantine Room, in her haste to reach Fuad's private apartment. She avoided the slow elevator with the Queen Nefertiti decor done by that effeminate Swiss interior designer — the one who had also designed Farouk's secret bedroom with the pink mirror on the ceiling that the stupid boy was so proud of, as well as his hidden library in which the fat little beast kept his collection of filthy erotica — until she finally burst into her brother's dressing room.

Fuad was trying on his Admiral's uniform in the centre of seven large cheval mirrors arranged in a circle. This enabled him to view himself from every possible angle, and he had been practising haughty expressions, with his lower jaw jutting out, just as he had seen in those newsreels of that arrogant Italian clown Mussolini. Now he was dithering over the question of whether his new cocked hat with the large green cockade with the letter 'F' embroidered in gold should be worn front to back, with the cockade on the left — as worn by the insolent British Admiral who at this very moment was probably getting drunk aboard the British flagship in Alexandria harbour and making stupid jokes at his expense — or sported from side to side with the cockade in front, as worn by the great Napoleon Buonaparte who, in spite of being quite a short man like himself, had a special kind of morose dignity. The hat was decidedly going to be a problem. Now, if he could only get

Napoleon's careworn stoop of the shoulders just right, together with the faraway expression of moody inner rage it would certainly create quite a memorable. . . no no, that might be seen as provocative by the British Ambassador who would give him another one of those humiliating lectures. On the other hand. . .

But his musings over important matters of State were violently interrupted:

"Murderer!"

He spun round, startled, in the direction of the intruder. It had been a hoarse strident cry, impossible to identify. Was it a man or a woman? God Almighty. . . this was the terrible moment he had always feared. . . a demented assassin with an irrational grievance. . . probably one of those disgruntled drunken fellahin, or worse, much worse, a member of that bunch of fanatics, the Moslem Brotherhood, whose sole objective was to depose him for some reason best known to themselves. How had the maniac got past the guards? Holy Spirits! Now he couldn't find his bearings with those accursed mirrors and the spotlights! Where was the door for God's sake? If only he could see the door he would be able to reach his small desk on the opposite side of the room and grab that loaded gold-plated Luger pistol that the German Ambassador had presented to him as a personal gift from that clever Adolf Hitler. . .

"You murderous imbecile. . . I only wish our father were alive, he would have you cut into little pieces and fed them to his pet cheetah. He would have castrated you and ordered his Nubian Guards to violate your concubines. He would have given you a tongue lashing that would have exploded that watermelon brain of yours. He would have broken. . ."

Suddenly aware that it was his crazy sister who was shouting at him — and, moreover, shouting with utter disregard for the fact that he was wearing the uniform of the Supreme Commander of the Royal Egyptian Fleet! — Fuad nervously tucked the palm of his right hand into his coat in a pose that he felt would combine a genuine hand-on-heart fraternal solicitude with chagrined dignity as portrayed in that lithograph of Napoleon standing in the snow following his defeat at the battle of Waterloo. Yes, that should give him the edge over her that he so badly needed in this unwelcome confrontation. His sister had always been so much quicker with words than he could ever be. She could speak four or five languages in the same breath when she was surrounded by those fawning foreign diplomats at embassy receptions, and it would make him look a fool. He hated that. But now she had slipped up and he had caught her out in her mistake. He would show her that he could be just as sharp for a change. He interrupted her triumphantly:

"Aha, it's *you* dear sister. So you have chosen to ignore the strict rule that female members of my Household are not authorized to trespass into my Royal Salamlek! You also seem to have overlooked the obvious fact that had I been cut into little pieces, as you say, I would hardly have been in any condition to hear one of our father's very boring homilies. Now would I? Besides, I also have to inform you that his Nubian Guards were all eunuchs, which would make their interest in my so-called concubines a trifle limited don't you think? And by the way what was all that nonsense about having me shot? Well, speak up Your Highness!"

He knew for sure that his reference to her conversation with that whore's son of an Assistant Chamberlain would shock her into silence and bring this unpleasant audience to an

end. He had not noticed that she had walked slowly half
way round the dimly lit back of the mirrors. Now he could
see her reflection in two of the mirrors as she stood behind
him with the Luger pistol that she had found in the open
drawer of his escritoire, and which she held up at eye level
in both hands, aimed steadily at his back. He turned round
slowly to face his sister, raised both his arms in a mock
gesture of surrender, and burst into loud wheezing laughter.

She looked puzzled: "You think it's funny? You don't think
I'll do it?"

He replied with a menacing expression: "I think it's funny,
yes. Because I know you *can't* do it"

"You think I can't do it? . . Why not?"

"Because the safety catch is on and the pistol cannot. . ."

"Thank you dear brother" she interrupted him calmly.

The bullet burst through his right testicle and thigh and
embedded itself in the mahogany shaft of the cheval mirror
behind him. He sucked his breath sharply through his teeth
with surprise but felt no pain from the wound as he keeled
over and lay motionless on his back on the carpet. It was
quite unlike the experience, seventeen years before, when
he had been shot in the throat by his enraged
brother-in-law, Prince Saphatin, simply because he had
divorced the fool's sister in order to marry the beautiful
Nazli. That wound had been excruciatingly painful right
away, and even after it had healed it still ached whenever
he shouted at his Ministers. And when he laughed it
sounded like a dog barking — not that he ever had much
to laugh about come to think of it. God, it was beginning
to hurt down there and it felt wet. . .

His sister was standing trembling and staring incredulously
at herself in one of the mirrors. There was no longer any
doubt in his mind that the wretched woman was decidedly

insane. He whispered something in her direction with a quiet courtesy that startled her out of the stunned reverie into which she appeared to have sought refuge.

All the anger had been drained out of her, and she suddenly felt very close to him. She did not want him to die after all. He looked so pitiful, so helpless lying there on his back. Not like a king at all. . . no. .·. more like that old stag she had shot on one of those desert night hunts. She had seen its eyes in the glare of the headlights as it lay dying and they had looked so wide and sad. . . not reproachful. . . it was almost as though the beast was feeling sorry for *her*. It had sickened her and she had vowed never to go on a hunt again. Now she felt she had broken that vow and she wanted to beg Fuad's forgiveness for it. But how could he have understood? What was he trying to say to her?

"Oh my poor brother, what did you say?"

"I said: You look very beautiful standing there my dearest. Now please call my physician before I bleed to death"

*   *   *

The Princess was, as we already know, banished from the Royal Household and confined to her modest palace down the road from our villa. I have assumed, not unreasonably, that she had been subjected all her life to the paralysing inertia of male dominance in a society in which, for example, an obese wife was as much a sign of a man's prosperity as the slender youthful figure of his mistress was evidence of his virility. It was a society, like others elsewhere, in which a woman could not own property or hold office, and in which she might only achieve some tenuous cajoling influence on her spouse or her master in

the bed-chamber if he were in the right frame of mind to
be beguiled.

It is likely that the Princess, with her superior education,
may have rebelled against these oppressive customs, and in
doing so, she would have breached the conventions in one
way or another, especially those of royal female conduct,
and caused frequent embarrassment and irritation in the
palace. That much is almost certain, otherwise she would
have been treated rather differently. She may also have felt
intolerably constrained, owing to her royal status, by being
relegated to the Haramlek, the women's wing of the Royal
Palace. It is also reasonable to suppose that she may have
been ahead of her time in holding certain radical views, and
that she was therefore not prepared to put up with the
conformity traditionally expected of a woman who, as
things stood at the time, should have no greater aspiration
than to have a husband and to be granted the privilege of
continuing to satisfy his needs for as long as possible until
he might tire of her. All else about the Princess would, of
course, be pure invention rather than conjecture, since it is
unlikely that there is in existence any detailed record of her
life history.

Kyriako and I used to walk past her palace on the way to
the beach. On one occasion, I had boasted to him that I
knew the Princess, and I described the incident when she
had offered me Turkish coffee, sweetmeats, and a Turkish
cigarette after catching me raiding her orchard. Perhaps my
later fantasies about her were partly engendered by that
childhood encounter.

Some years ago, I hazily recall, the information came my
way — but I cannot remember how — that an Egyptian
Princess had died from shock at the age of ninety-two in
Lausanne, Switzerland, following an attack of paroxysmal

coughing after accidentally ingesting very hot Turkish coffee into her lungs.

The other Princess, my lost love who became a Queen for a while, eventually remarried, moved to St Moritz, Switzerland, and, for all I know, lived happily ever after.

Which is how a fairy tale about a Princess should end.

The Collector

I had been told by my father that Julius Caesar's Roman army of occupation had been billeted along the coast at Alexandria about two thousand years ago. Now the only reminder was a tram station named Camp de César, a few stops up the line from Palais. But it was not quite the *only* reminder as it happens, because one day I found an old Roman coin on the piece of waste ground near the convent when I was kicking the ball around with the Bedouin children.

It did not look like a coin at first because it was caked with a hard layer of clay. It looked more like a small disk-shaped pebble. That is probably why I picked it up. . . I was always picking things up off the ground. Once I had picked up a mysterious pure white object shaped like a small sausage and taken it home to show to Mahroos. He told me to throw it away at once because it was a piece of dried up dog excrement and therefore of no possible use to anyone. And, besides, he did not believe that my mother would consider a sunbaked dog's turd a suitable thing to bring into the house and that even if I hid it in my bedroom it would eventually be found and he would be blamed. I obeyed Mahroos because the object had disintegrated in my hand and I had by now completely lost interest in it anyway.

But the object I discovered that day was certainly quite different. It was heavier than a pebble, and when I spat on it and rubbed off some of the clay with my thumb nail,

revealing the green patina underneath, I noticed that there
was the clear image in relief of a human portrait in profile
on the newly exposed surface. I took the small metal object
home and scrubbed it with my father's nail brush — which
my father found very distressing when he discovered the
soiled brush because, as he later explained to me, it was
genuine hog's bristle and it had been undoubtedly ruined
for ever and that such conduct was incomprehensible. That
was the phrase he had used: *'Votre conduite est
incompréhensible'*. He was always very polite even when
he was angry. It would never have occurred to him, he
added sadly, to lay a finger on his own father's nail brush,
and he hoped that there would not be a repetition of such
flagrant abuse of one of his personal belongings because he
would now have to bring the incident to the attention of my
mother for whatever punishment she deemed fit.

After drying the coin on my shirt-tail — I am beginning to
remember the details very clearly now — I saw what was
some kind of bird modelled in relief on the other side.
There was also some lettering on both sides of the coin, but
it was worn and hard to make out. My father kept a bottle
of battery acid in the garage and he had shown me once
that if you dropped a copper coin in a small cup containing
some of the acid, it would froth up and come out as shiny
as new. I had been so impressed by that demonstration that
I had not paid the slightest attention to his warning that I
must. . . *'never ever, do you understand my boy, never in
any circumstances whatsoever go anywhere near the bottle
of acid. Vous comprenez?*

I must have inadvertently overlooked his added warning
that he would, in all conscience, not be answerable for the
consequences of my disobedience, because I cleaned the
Roman coin in a cupful of his acid and it came up as bright
as a newly cast gold ingot. I then put a lot of energy into

raising a high polish on it with a yellow duster and Brasso that I borrowed from the kitchen cupboard. I did the same thing to all the coins I discovered over the next few months — except that I used my mother's toothbrush instead of my father's nail brush for the early stages of cleaning. Of course I did not show my treasured collection to anyone other than Mahroos who was most impressed and who praised me for having found much more worthwhile things to pick up than dog's muck.

It was not until several years later that I made an equally, if not more important discovery: I had totally and irreversibly ruined a valuable collection of ancient artifacts in the innocent certainty that I had improved their appearance beyond measure. Strangely enough, either of these facts is valid, depending almost entirely on one's point of view.

And over the years I was to observe or come into direct contact with many different kinds of collectors. I gave much thought to the phenomenon of collecting and to its origins. I considered, too, the mysterious and powerful force behind the impulse to put together and to own categories of objects. What is it, I wondered, that sparks off this often obsessive need to collect that sometimes drives humans to acts of cruelty and of self-destruction as well as to crime, and even to murder?

Naturally there is also a constructive side to collecting: the enjoyment of the objects themselves; or the academic interest in examining them and in forming a coherent assemblage for a scientific purpose; or the collection may be exclusively a form of investment, and there's nothing much wrong with that. However, this merely describes the act and superficial reason for collecting. . . but surely the underlying motivation goes deeper than that?

There is a species of bird in which the unusually dull plumaged cock collects brightly coloured objects and places them along the entrance to and within the interior of his bower. He does this in order to lure the even duller-looking hen bird into his mating chamber where he dances around her pointing eagerly with his beak at certain choice items in his collection. She is not always sufficiently impressed, by the way, to allow him to consummate his elaborate plans for passing on his genes to future generations. She may casually walk out to find another cock with a more imaginative and eye-catching display. Collecting, needless to say, is very much a matter of personal taste.

And now I remember a very special man, one of the first collectors whom I encountered — and there have been many throughout my life. I should like to tell his story because I don't think that anyone else remembers him after half a century, and perhaps he should not be entirely forgotten.

*   *   *

I could see his house from Madame Kyriakides' balcony. It was at the top of the incline at the far end of the area of waste ground next to the convent. He used to wave to me in a friendly way when he visited the grocer below to do his shopping every Saturday afternoon.

It was shortly after I had been allowed to live at home that I was able to sneak away and wait to greet him outside the grocer's shop. My mother would have been horrified by my innocent imprudence. In any event, there would have been nothing to fear because the man had a single obsessive interest in life that was all-consuming and which left no room for deviations of any kind whatsoever.

When I greeted him as he left the shop, he responded with solemn politeness and an invitation to accompany him to his house where I might care to join him in drinking some fresh lemonade he would prepare with the lemons he had just purchased.

He lived alone in that small three-roomed house. It was bare of furniture apart from a square pine table and three green painted bentwood chairs in the kitchen that also served as the dining room. The bedroom contained a small tubular steel folding bed and a wardrobe painted in the same green colour as the kitchen chairs. There was a small shower room and lavatory which smelt quite strongly of olive-oil-based laundry soap and urine.

He always wore a blue beret and I noticed that he did not remove it indoors, and I briefly wondered if it had a different shape when he wore it in bed and if it got soggy when he was taking a shower. But the thing that struck me most about the beret was that he wore it vertically on his head with patriarchal dignity, rather like ecclesiastical headgear, and not flattened down one side as I had seen Kyriako wear his beret when we went for our occasional walks on Sundays.

Later, while we were sipping our cold drinks, he asked me what had been the purpose in my spending so much time on the balcony above the grocer's shop. After I repeated the explanation given to me by my father, he placed the fingertips of his right hand lightly and hesitantly on my cheek for a brief moment. He had the same look of sadness that I had seen in my father's eyes and I could not understand it.

When I had finished my drink he asked me if I might possibly be interested in seeing his collection and that it would give him much pleasure if I would be kind enough to view it with his guidance. He was as polite as my father.

The room we entered was lined with shelves from floor to ceiling on all four walls — there were even three rows of shelves above the door. It was cooler than the other two rooms because the slatted wooden shutters were always kept closed, and that made it seem cloistered and mysterious in some way. It was the very heart of the house. It was where he displayed his collection of canned fish.

The shelves in that darkened room were stacked with cans. I noticed right away that no two cans were the same and that they all bore labels that faced the front so that they could be read without having to be rotated.

As I walked along the rows the man would pick one off a shelf, place it gently in my hand as though it were a precious and fragile work of art — the way my father had once done with the small Japanese ivory carvings he kept on the chest of drawers in his bedroom — and then he would explain to me why it was such a rare item.

He told me that the English word *'can'* was short for canister and that it was derived from the Greek word *'Kanastron'* which meant *'basket of reeds'*. He was proud of that, he added, because he was Greek, and there was no doubt that the English would have had some difficulty in finding such a satisfactory word as 'can' if it had not been for the elegance and ingenuity of the Greek language. That made a great deal of sense to me at the time — and still does. I have since discovered that in the year 1795 the French government offered a prize of 10,000 francs for a method of food preservation and that it was won in 1810 by Nicolas François Appert, a Parisian confectioner, who used glass bottles kept in boiling water. That was fifty years before Louis Pasteur discovered that it was very small organisms that were the cause of food spoilage. Monsieur Appert wrote a treatise entitled: 'Art de Conserver les Substances Animales et Végétales'. He was my friend's

hero and his framed engraved portrait hung in the bedroom
with a portrait of the collector's mother on one side and
another engraving of a statue of a naked youth throwing a
discus on the other.

You can appreciate now that cans are not merely the
containers for food we take for granted, but that they have
a history of their own. William Parry the English Arctic
explorer, for instance, left some cans of roast veal with
carrots and gravy in the Arctic during the third expedition
in search of the Northwest Passage in 1824. Some of the
cans were opened in 1911 and the contents were found to
be fresh and palatable. How astonishing that must have
seemed at the time. Everyone must have wondered how that
was possible. Well, in 1818, Mr Donkin and Mr Hall coated
iron cans with tin, and so the contents did not corrode the
interior. No wonder my friend found cans so interesting.
But why did he collect canned fish?

The explanation is a simple one: some people collect wines,
and they treasure the bottles in their cellars, especially the
rare ones — the ones that have matured to the stage where
they have reached a peak of exquisite fragrance. Sometimes
a rare bottle is never uncorked, and it may be sold at
auction for a very large sum of money. The wine in it may
be sour and undrinkable, but the bottle, with its identifying
label of origin, is still eagerly acquired by a collector who
will add it proudly to his cellar. If the wine is in prime
condition and ready to be drunk, the collector will perform
the customary ritual of allowing the sediment to reach the
bottom of the bottle and the wine to reach room
temperature before testing it with his nose and savouring it
with his palate.

My friend explained to me that the fish in the cans matured
in the same way as wine. If the quality was of the highest,
then the maturation of the contents would justify the

collector's patience and reward his discerning taste with the
flavours imbued by time alone. Some cans were of priceless
historical value: one of the most treasured items in his
collection was a can of pilchard in a piquant spiced sauce
that had been on William Parry's expedition. The white
unadorned label was aged but intact and it reminded me of
the most valuable franked and unperforated postage stamp
in my father's collection. The man informed me solemnly
that he would not part with that unique item for all the
caviar in the Black Sea.

"But how do you know if it is any good to eat?" I had asked
him innocently. He looked at me with a benevolent smile
and replied: "You will learn one day, my little friend, that
some things in life are a delight to the eyes and heart but
that they can destroy if they are unwisely taken"

He then picked up a flat oblong can from another shelf and
whispered: "Portuguese. Yes, a very good year". He opened
the can carefully and placed it on the table. "It is not ready
yet" he said "we must wait for a while for the fish to
breathe. . . you understand. . . the flavour has been trapped
for many years and now it must be released"

I do not believe that I have ever tasted anything that
surpassed the flavour of those sardines served on a chipped
plate with great ceremony by Monsieur Dimitri Kitrilakis.

The Virgin

I had been told by the nuns more than once, not only that:
'*Our Lord Jesus Christ is perfect*' but also that: '*The Holy
Virgin, His Mother, is perfect*'. I somehow already knew
that God The Father, is *even more perfect*. It was quite easy
to imagine all three in their perfection, because I remember
seeing all those pictures of them, including the coloured
statues of Jesus and of The Virgin Mary. I did not see any
pictures of God, though, until I went to Florence in Italy.
But that was when I was quite a bit older and had already
made up my mind about, among other things, God, as well
as Perfection, Purity, Love — and virginity.

Yes, Jesus certainly looked convincingly perfect in the
pictures. He was always dressed in spotless white sheets,
just as the ancient Romans wore, with lots of folds. . .
especially with the long folded bit over one arm, which
must have made it very awkward to do things properly
when you need both arms free, like catching a ball for
instance, or climbing a tree or chasing a cat or jumping
onto a moving tram. Perhaps he took his sheets off to do
that.

I had seen his pictures in a book when I was taken to visit
my grandmother. Jesus had worn a nice ghallabeya in a few
of the pictures the nuns had shown me — it was like the
one Mahroos wore on his days off when he travelled to his
village. My favourite picture, hanging in the convent dining
room, was the one where Jesus was crouched on one knee

telling his friends a story. It must have been a wonderful story because he was pointing his finger toward some mountains far away, and his friends had their eyes wide open as they stared at him. Yes, and he was wearing a different ghallabeya with embroidered edging, like the one worn by the Travelling Teller of Tales. Maybe Jesus was also a Travelling Teller of Tales. He, too, seemed to do a lot of travelling because he was in a different place in every picture.

There was one that I found particularly interesting — where he was very angry, overturning tables and throwing things on the floor of this big building with lots of pillars. He was surrounded by quite a large crowd of people wearing ghallabeyas and looking alarmed, and in one corner there was a small group of men, dressed in black cloaks, who were obviously not pleased with what he was doing because they were huddled together and pointing at him with their backs turned away. They looked like the grim-faced priests who visited the convent occasionally, the ones who upset the Mother Superior, because I had noticed on one occasion that she was blushing and her lips were closed very tight when the men were frowning and talking to her sharply in whispers. One of them had prodded, with his crooked finger, the big ebony cross with the polished silver Jesus that was hanging down on her chest. I think that had really annoyed her.

Yes, it was clear to me that you could get angry if you were Jesus, and throw things down and you could still be a good person. . . but only if the people whose things you were throwing down had done something bad. So that made it all right. But it was still a bit confusing, because the picture didn't explain what bad things those people had done. The nuns informed me briefly that the bad people were selling their goods and dealing with money in the temple. So perhaps Jesus had been annoyed because the goods were too expensive, like my father had been when he arrived home one day and told my mother that he was certainly not prepared to pay five piasters for half a kilo of imported apples he had seen in the town, however nice and juicy and crisp they looked. They also looked fresh, shiny and red and were probably very sweet, he added in order to emphasize his obvious annoyance over the price. So I asked him if he had thrown the apples on the ground just like Jesus. My father considered my question carefully for some time and, after adjusting his pince-nez a little further up the bridge of his nose, replied that if Jesus had done anything like that, although he could not recall any such odd incident being mentioned in the New Testament, it was not surprising, and he quite understood Jesus's feelings in the circumstances.

My mother was even more annoyed, because she turned to me with that beautiful smile of hers that always gave me a wonderfully cool feeling of well-being and explained that she was particularly fond of apples and had not tasted one since she had left France, and that it was on occasions like this that she regretted leaving her beloved France because she found the climate in Egypt debilitating and it gave her migraines. My father did not bring up the subject of apples ever again in my presence, but a few days later he and Mahroos planted, next to the grapefruit tree in the orchard outside the kitchen, a solitary apple tree that somehow never bore fruit — at least, not while we lived there.

'Perhaps you will understand about Jesus and the Holy Mother when you are a bit older'. That's what the nuns had suggested helpfully. In the meanwhile, they said, I must pray to Him to make me a good boy. That was a problem, because I was not aware of being a bad boy, except when I upset my mother of course. And I was always very sorry

about it afterwards. I didn't know where Jesus was, so I used to pretend that he was walking past the bedroom window and I would ask him to make me a good boy and would He please stop me from upsetting my mother because I only knew that I had upset her after I had been told by my father that I had done so. By then it would be too late. Jesus obviously couldn't have heard me because my mother continued to be upset by a lot of the things that I did without realizing at the time that they would upset her, such as pissing on our Scots terrier, Mirza, because it made Mahroos laugh. She had later described my conduct as *'dégueulasse'* to my father. It means *filthy and disgusting* in French and it instantly became my favourite epithet that I frequently repeated with great gusto in the presence of members of the family and their friends, much to my father's dismay.

Once, Mahroos refused to let me pick all the ripe lemons off the tree in our garden to give to Mabrooka, but I had picked the lemons all the same and thrown them at him — as, no doubt, Jesus would have done. My mother, who had witnessed my display of bad temper, told me that I was a very bad boy and later informed my father reproachfully that his son's *'conduite atroce'* was, without a doubt, another trait that had been inherited from his side of the family. It was very confusing indeed.

There was also the question of Saint Joseph, who, in the pictures, was either walking alongside the Virgin Mary, who was riding side-saddle on a donkey, or planing a plank of wood at a carpenter's bench — except, that is, when he was in the stable standing amiably behind the Virgin Mary who was stooping over the manger in which the baby Jesus lay naked without a blanket over him. This seemed rather imprudent to me at the time, because it could get very cold at night, especially at Christmas.

Well, the question of the precise nature of Saint Joseph's relationship with Jesus Christ was another one of my questions that I thought the nuns had answered somewhat ambiguously. Because if Saint Joseph was Jesus's father, how could God be his father as well, I insisted. And which one bought Jesus's ghallabeya for him, and the nice pair of sandals he sometimes wore? And if God loved Jesus, and Jesus was his son, and if God was so powerful, then why didn't he stop the Romans from crucifying his only son. . . *Mais alors, pourquoi pas*?

Some of the nuns smiled at the silliness of my questions while the rest shook their heads and made the sign of the cross. 'Well, you see' they explained patiently 'Saint Joseph was not the *REAL* father of Jesus. Was Jesus an orphan? Where did you hear that? No no no, Jesus was not an orphan and so you see, he was not *adopted* by Saint Joseph. He was the Son of God. Ah, and you want to know about the Holy Mary? Well, She was the Mother of God. Yes yes, and our Lord Jesus was her son of course'. I knew what an orphan was, but they had to explain to me what 'adopted' meant before we could move on, as I hoped, to an explanation of the bewildering illogicality of it all. As soon as we got to the part where The Holy Mother was a Virgin — and I was naturally very curious to know what a virgin was — they appeared to run into some major difficulty as they cast their eyes heavenward and muttered the word 'virgin' several times, clearly searching for some divine guidance as to how to explain this ineffable concept to the little boy in a way that would avoid further importunate interrogation on his part.

The question was quickly set aside when one of the younger nuns burst into uncontrollable giggles and was ordered to go straight to her dormitory and told that she would be dealt with later by Mother Superior. Her giggling stopped abruptly and her right hand now grappled with the lower part of her face as though preventing some loathsome creature from escaping out of her mouth, while her left hand gripped her crucifix in frantic desperation. Her eyes were watering and wide with humiliation and panic, when she suddenly burst into tears before pulling her robe above her ankles as she rushed out of the room with a loud clattering of her metal-studded black boots on the waxed floorboards. Yes, I remember all those details, especially the black boots.

The other nuns appeared stunned by what had just happened, and one of them bit the knuckle of her thumb so hard that she let out a cry of pain. Another nun fell to her knees and seemed to be muttering words in supplication at the ceiling while an elderly nun was moaning *'deus misereatur'*.

Bewildered by these startling events, I was now more interested than ever to discover the meaning of the word 'virgin' and all its implications — which were dramatic enough to have caused such emotional disconcert among those normally sedate nuns.

Later that day I made the tactless error of asking my mother the meaning of the word *'vierge'*. My mother hastily brushed my enquiry aside while expressing mild irritation with the nuns for bringing up such an indelicate subject in the presence of a little boy. It was *'une inconvenance insupportable'*. In any case, she added with a sigh before retiring to her room to lie down for a while on her chaise-longue with a mild migraine as a result of my tiresome questioning, the conduct of the nuns was bound to be a little peculiar, since they had chosen voluntarily to live such a sterile closeted existence.

I was, by this time, more intrigued than ever by that mysterious word. And was there a connection between 'perfect' and 'virgin'? I had to know.

It was no good asking Mahroos. He might perhaps have revealed everything to me, if I had only known the Arabic word for 'virgin' and therefore been able to broach the subject. But, oddly enough, it was Mahroos who would unwittingly and indirectly be the instrument of my enlightenment — at least where the baffling enigma regarding virginity was concerned — and sooner than I expected.

Mahroos had known his bride-to-be since they were children. Their marriage had almost certainly been arranged, and the terms agreed between their two families, soon after the girl child was born.

Sanniya was now fourteen years old and, as far as everyone was concerned, ready for the nuptial bed. Everyone, that is, with the exception of Sanniya herself, whom no-one had consulted regarding her personal views about her preparedness — or otherwise — for marriage; her readiness to start bearing children; her feelings; her emotions and, least of all, her ignorance and fears of what it was all about. Nor, for that matter, would her consent to commit herself for life to her husband-to-be have been sought by anyone. And above all, Sanniya would never have dreamed of questioning, let alone of opposing her father's wishes. Was it not the same all over the world? Did young girls — apart from a privileged wealthy few, like Haroun Pasha's daughters who went to far away schools where there were mountains covered in snow and who would probably marry rich foreigners — apart from them, did ordinary nubile young girls truly have a choice?

To remain unwedded after reaching a certain age was evidence of some ugly concealed disability, was it not?

Even those devoted spinsters — like Abu Hassan's skinny
daughter whom everyone called Mishmish and who had
remained unblessed by marriage in order to minister to the
needs of her widowed father — even such worthy women
were looked at askance and treated with some suspicion.
Do you know why they called her Mishmish? Because
'bookrah fi'l mishmish' means 'tomorrow in the apricots'
in Arabic, which was another way of saying: 'it will never
happen to her'. Everyone knew what *that* meant, just as
they knew that she seemed at times to be possessed by the
devil of perverseness and arrogance. For how else was it
possible for her to enjoy such a fallow existence, deprived
of the comfort of a husband, however obtuse, abusive,
coarse, violent, evil-smelling and carnally rough he may be,
and however repulsive his physical appearance. And to
make matters worse, Mishmish had often been heard
singing cheerfully and laughing to herself as she went about
her chores. It was truly unnatural and most provocative. It
was not until she had been mocked once too often by the
men and shouted at in the street by some of the wives and
called a whore, threatened, and warned to keep away from
their husbands that she had finally covered herself fully and
hidden her face in public and stopped singing and laughing
out loud and dyeing her feet with henna.

And what other reasons could there be for some girls not
to marry? Could it be some hint of a shameful past that
made the poor creature unfit for marriage unless
accompanied by a dowry of such inflated proportions that
it would surely be better if the wretched girl's life were to
be mercifully and swiftly ended by a fatal consumption or
fever?

I felt I was getting no closer to solving the mystery after
having gleaned some bizarre information from Mahroos and
from Mabrooka. Devoted spinsters? Shameful past? What

could it all mean? Abu Bakr himself had replied to my inarticulate enquiry by explaining with great seriousness and much solemn stroking of his moustache, and with an occasional nod and wink in the direction of his two wives who happened to be in attendance, that there existed a precious asset, bestowed upon womanhood by Allah himself, which transcended mere beauty. It was a jewel treasured above all other values in a bride: it was her Purity, securely locked in her chastity and untouched by any man — safely preserved for the bridegroom, like a comb of sweetest honey, by an unbroken and sacred natural seal. Yes, she may be uncomely, ungainly, her complexion pitted with chicken-pox scars, bucktoothed, hatchet-faced, big-eared, narrow of hip, thin of breast and foul of breath — yet with her purity intact, and demonstrably so at the crucial moment, she would not be disqualified from having the blessing of marriage bestowed upon her, even if it meant her existing gratefully and unquestioningly at the most menial level in the hierarchy of a husband's assembly of wives. For such is the Dictate of Nature herself bowing to the Will of Allah.

Purity intact? What did *that* mean? I mean, what did it mean *precisely*? Was I getting warmer? *Jewel? Sacred honey? Natural seal?* What had they got to do with *anything*? Why had the nuns not mentioned any of these things? Did Abu Bakr know something that the nuns were unaware of? Moreover, were the nuns and Abu Bakr talking about the same thing? Perhaps not. No. In fact I still didn't seem to be getting any closer to understanding virginity, especially in connection with The Holy Virgin Mary Mother of God and also of our Lord Jesus Christ who was also the Son of God. It was obviously one of those peculiar riddles, like the one in the song about how you can be your own grandfather, only much more difficult to figure out.

On top of all that, there was the Holy Ghost. He was the one who caused the greatest difficulty when it came to explanations. And still does. So we'll leave him out of this story altogether because it's getting complicated enough as it is, and he didn't appear to have any connection with my enquiries. Besides, you don't hear all that much said about the Holy Ghost nowadays. Although frankly, in my opinion (which you may or may not be interested in, how am I to know?) I think he may turn out to be the most meaningful and helpful one of the lot in the long run. That is, as far as human spirituality is concerned. But I'm digressing again.

* * *

We now arrive at the day when Mahroos finally weds his childhood sweetheart to whom he has been betrothed since Sanniya was one year old and he was thirteen. As I said earlier, she is now fourteen years old, and, in any event, it has taken all this time for the appropriate and long-agreed dowry to be saved piaster by piaster, and put by.

The celebrations were to take place at Mahroos's village and we had all been invited to attend as honoured guests. My mother was unfortunately unable to attend owing to a severe last minute migraine brought on by the thought of all the noise, the quite dreadful and unhygienic food that she would be expected to eat which would undoubtedly afflict us all with dysentery, not to mention the nauseating open drains, the intolerable heat and the abominable flies, all of which the mad natives apparently seemed actually to find 'ravissant'. It was 'incroyable'. And yet, about a year later, when Mahroos and Sanniya brought their first baby to my mother when it was very sick and covered in purulent lesions, she immediately took charge. She swabbed the tiny creature's sores clean with great tenderness and nursed it back to health, uncomplaining and with loving care, for several weeks. My father was dazzled, as he would be for the rest of his life, by my mother's apparently wholly logical inconsistency.

I was to be accompanied to the wedding and watched with the greatest vigilance by my mother's young sister Frida, my beautiful young Tantine Frida, who had been brought over from France to stay with us for a few months to help around the house, but mainly to look after me because I was a truly problematical little boy who had picked up those wild habits from the savage Bedouins and it was all too distressing for a person of my mother's sensitivity to have to cope with on her own in this uncivilized country that was so unlike her beloved France. We were all very concerned about my mother's sensitivity.

We set off early in the morning, my father, Frida and I, in the red Fiat touring Sedan car with the canvas top. My mother had forced him to buy the car after the accident with his motorcycle when the sidecar in which I was sitting became detached after he had crashed into a tree. This had all been caused by the vehicle bouncing off a donkey that had suddenly decided to stray into the middle of the road across his path. The donkey had raced off in one direction, while the sidecar had gone careening in the opposite direction into the canal with me, together with ten kilos of sugar cubes in brown paper bags my father had purchased wholesale. The sidecar had remained afloat and drifted a short distance downstream before coming to rest among some reeds. I had survived the accident a little frightened but unscathed, and sucking a sugar cube when I was rescued by fellahin labourers who were hauling a barge by rope along the towpath.

My father, who had fractured his left arm and temporarily lost consciousness, was taken by a passing motorist to the

Italian Hospital. To make matters worse, as he later complained to my mother, he had also broken his pince-nez as a result of the mishap.

I eventually found my way home, as I recall, with one sandal missing, a bump on my head, and my pockets stuffed with soggy sugar cubes. My mother had been very upset and as a result suffered an exceptionally severe migraine, especially with the shock coming so soon after the time Tantine Frida had been thrown off the back of the motorcycle when it had gone over a bump in the road. Her derrière had, it appears, been badly bruised, and my mother had been greatly irritated by my father's carelessness in failing to notice her sister's disappearance until he had arrived home and had a cup of tea. The motorcycle (which, incidentally, had been undamaged by the latest fracas with the donkey — apart from a few dents, a sheared throttle pedal and a bent handlebar) finally had to go. To disappear. Permanently. She did not wish to set eyes on it ever again.

This vexed my father because, as he told me many years later, it was a superb chromium plated Brough Superior, the aristocrat of motorcycles, which had been tuned to his touch like a Stradivarius violin. He had always been very attached to it, in a manner of speaking. Indeed, it had been a stroke of bad luck that the donkey with whom he had collided had not been similarly tuned, he had added with a smile. My father had always had a highly developed appreciation for the more subtle ironies of life.

We arrived at Mahroos's village to a tumultuous welcome, each of the grinning male adults insisting on giving the Klaxon motor horn a vigorous squeeze in order to produce sounds that drew shrieks of derisive laughter from all the womenfolk, since those honkings clearly reminded them of the anal trumpetings of proud men and other beasts. On any other occasion it would have been the highlight of the village week, but this, let us remember, was a wedding day, and so we moved on to greater and more important happenings.

Shortly after our arrival two fattened sheep were slaughtered, skinned, and butchered to fit the large brass pots in which salted spiced water was bubbling. The pots fitted over the open tops of mud ovens that were fuelled with flattened sun-dried cow pats. Far from being unpleasant, the smoke from the smouldering dung had an exquisite aroma — the kind of smell, I was to discover many years later in England, that one gets from an autumn bonfire on which pine cones and wet leaves have been thrown. It whetted the appetite for the delicacies that the women started to serve as soon as we were seated cross-legged in the large carpeted tent reserved for the bride's and the groom's families and their special guests.

I remember in particular helping myself to a portion of steamed flaky pastry, interleaved with slivers of tender goose meat, which I devoured greedily under the watchful gaze of Tantine Frida; and how I then picked up a slice of ice-cold watermelon with my oily fingers and buried my face in its cool sweet watery flesh to slake my thirst. Low tables all around us were loaded with meatball kuftas with rice; stuffed vine-leaves spiced with dill seed; raw tomatoes with fresh parsley and basil; sliced onion, olives, chickpeas, pickles and goat milk cheese; hollow cracked-wheat kubbebas with pine kernels and minced lamb filling spiced with cumin and cinnamon; roast chicken basted with clarified butter-oil and black pepper; sweet-corn cobs and quails grilled over charcoal; hard-boiled eggs; sesame seed tahina paste with crushed garlic in which to dip freshly baked coarse bread, gritty with millstone dust; eggplant and okra spicy stews; broiled sweet potatoes; sliced cucumber in sour cream; fresh kos lettuce, large green capsicums, radishes and raw chilies. There were rose-coloured *sharbaat* iced drinks with nuts floating in them; beakers of lemonade; bowls of sugared almonds; dishes of candied flower petals and orange slices; platters of deep fried paper-thin pastry ba'lawa and vermicelli konafa stuffed with minced fruit and nuts and soaked in syrup; dainty baskets of dried figs, dates, and apricots; huge piles of shortbread biscuits and pistachio nut sugar wafers; mangoes, melons, custard apples (called *'ishtah'* because of the soft white texture of the flesh, and which means *'cream'* in Arabic), guavas, bananas, satsumas, sugar-cane, persimmons, pomegranates, and crisp red raw dates.

I knew nothing of the moment everyone was eagerly awaiting at the end of the day as I gorged myself on a mouthful of food from every delectable dish. If I have reminisced in great detail over the wedding banquet, it may only be because I am instinctively conscious of the fact that food is the primary and more urgent requirement for the survival of the individual of the species, while the mechanism of procreation can usually take place at leisure in the fullness of time. This is, let's face it, a question of priorities. It was not long before I fell fast asleep, my stomach distended like an overfed puppy's, on a large cushion in a corner of the tent.

In mid-afternoon I woke up full of renewed energy and joined the other children in their rumbustious games. My only pair of patent leather shoes was badly scuffed, my black velvet short pants were torn at the hip, and the tail of my silk blouse was inexplicably scorched. It didn't seem to matter at the time, with all the celebrations and music and games going on.

But Tantine Frida, I recall, was tearfully reproached by my mother on our return home for her inability to acquit herself of her responsibilities to her elder sister by failing to ensure

that her only son was returned to her in an acceptable
condition. In other words, as clean and impeccably attired
as he had left the house that morning. She had, she added,
given her young sister nothing but kindness, not to mention
— the facts must be faced — charity. Frida, sharply brought
down to earth and with her lower lip trembling with
remorse, was reminded of the wilful neglect of the trust
placed in her together with her incomprehensible disregard,
in the present circumstances, for the honour of their family.
Words were not to be minced on this painful occasion, and
nor were hypocrisy and pretence permitted to obscure the
truth, she was told more in sadness than in anger. And as
for the cherished memory of their beloved father, Honoré
Sapet — who had so very nearly given his life to his
country, and whose honour, as befitted his name, would
remain for ever untarnished by shame — my mother was,
she finally announced, *'privé de la parole'*, which means
'speechless' in French. This was truly a rare condition for
my mother to be afflicted with and I made a mental note at
the time to find out a little more, at the appropriate
moment, about the precise nature of Tantine Frida's
delinquencies, especially with regard to their father, who
had died many years before I was born, and what his
connection with my dishevelled state might possibly be.

I mention, only in passing, that the appropriate moment
never presented itself because one evening after dinner in
Tantine Frida's apartment in the Rue de la Sorbonne in
Paris, about half a century later, it became clear that she
had entirely forgotten that unhappy episode with my
mother. She had, by the way, prepared a meal for the two
of us of thinly sliced bulls' testes in beurre noire, served
with a side plate of endives au gratin, with freshly baked
crusty French bread. The young claret was light and with a
character entirely compatible with the finesse of that most

delicious dish. . . but I'm digressing. What she *did* remember, as clearly as I did, after all these years, was the long-awaited concluding event of that memorable wedding day.

Now, all the while, the mutton had been boiling in its bouillon of spices and herbs. . . for freshly killed meat is always tough unless it is boiled tender. It was to go on cooking all day and most of the evening, until the special event took place. The climactic nuptial initiatory rite would be followed by the raucous congratulatory yelling of the men and the joyful ululations of the women. And only then would the tender meat be served and eagerly devoured by the assembly — the sheep's heads, with their cheeks, brains, tongues, eyes, and jellified skin and fat being placed before the honoured guests. My plump Tantine Frida and I feasted ourselves on these privileged delicacies in a tacit compact of blissful gluttony under my father's glances of benign incredulity.

But first. . . first we had to witness the most important moment of all: the whole village and visiting guests had quickly assembled outside the closed window of the room that was to be the bridal chamber and from which we all heard a loud long drawn out scream. A few seconds later a shutter in that window opened just wide enough for a hand to appear. It fluttered, briefly, for our benefit, a square of white linen with a lace border before withdrawing back into the room. The linen was stained with fresh crimson blood. There was a fleeting moment of breathless silence. . . and then pandemonium suddenly broke out as everyone celebrated the triumphant evidence that had just been displayed.

Mahroos, who had been standing next to me at the time and gripping my hand sweatily, now had tears streaming down his cheeks as he was hugged and congratulated by all the men.

Bewildered, I asked Tantine Frida what had happened. *Tantine, Tantine. . . tell me. . . what was it all about?* And she replied calmly: "The midwife cut the throat of the pigeon, you see, to show everyone that the bride was pure. . . that she was a virgin"

Pigeon? Virgin? I was aware that the Arabic vernacular word for the secret part of a woman most joked about and at the same time most sought after by men was sometimes referred to as a pigeon! And the bizarre reason why it had to have its throat cut amid such boisterous jubilation was not altogether unfamiliar, for after all, did not the Bedouin Ibn Mahmood cut the throats of creatures with great ceremony? So now there was a palpable connection between Virginity and that hidden Object of Desire. . . and the cutting of throats.

But there were still some mysteries, a number of loose strands that would eventually need to be pulled together. The Holy Virgin, for instance, may turn out to be a problem, and the link with the white pigeon with the twig in its beak that hovered among the angels in many of the pictures required some explanation. Yes, and was Saint Joseph like Ibn Mahmood? That made some sense, presumably. But Jesus Christ? And God? And Love and Purity and Perfection? There was obviously much more to discover and it was not going to be easy. Nevertheless, I was convinced that I was on the right track at last.

The Old Trouper

Mahroos, it so happens, was not entirely familiar with the Bedouin dialect, and I would sometimes tease him by using naughty phrases I had learned from the older boys — usually without understanding their full meaning. The neighbouring Nubian gardener further enriched my vocabulary of colourful invective with a choice repertoire in his own melodious tongue. Mahroos would certainly have made a fair guess at the meaning of all these elaborately obscene expressions, and he would face the dilemma of whether or not to reprimand me, because he knew that I was, in turn, bound to start asking for specific explanations and then — Allah be merciful! — the little rascal's mother would somehow doubtless get involved. All he wanted was peace and quiet and not to be involved in any upsets, that was all. And so he would bite his tongue and get down to some hard digging and clearing in that corner of the garden where the wretched builders had buried all their rubble instead of carting it away as they were supposed to have done and he would plant the new loquat, persimmon and medlar saplings and mix plenty of well-rotted chicken manure in the soil and they would bear fruit in no time at all. And then the master would be pleased.

The Teller of Tales hardly ever used coarse language — unless he was quoting an unsavoury character in a tale — no, he was far too subtle and dignified for that. He hatched puns and innuendo, he nested layer upon layer of meaning, often beyond the perception of many in his audience. This does not mean that he was ever obscure to the point of losing their attention for a single moment. It simply means that he did not always play to the gallery. He would sometimes craftily aim an obscure witticism at a selected member of the audience whose perceptive reaction, a glance of recognition, would be the Teller's special reward — perhaps more satisfying to him at that moment than the noisy bursts of appreciation he received from all the others on another level of humour.

It was a particular example of the many mysterious touches of human intercourse that I was to experience and wonder at as, over the years, I groped my way erratically toward adulthood. And it took a good many more years for me to come to the realisation that it is unwise to expect universal approval of one's actions or achievements — this can only lead to bitter disappointment. An understanding and appreciative audience of just one can be a most precious thing.

I also came to realize that childhood is a precious thing: not to be deprived of or abandoned a single moment too soon — if ever. There is a great difference between behaving childishly and preserving a child-like quality throughout life. It may be the greatest tragedy of our lives to lose all of the fresh insight and purity of spirit with which we were endowed in our infancy.

I never lost my appetite for wild stories that had first been aroused by the Teller of Tales. As I grew older, I turned eagerly to other tellers of tales: to the writers of books and of plays, and to the theatre and the movies. I made up my own stories, and when I grew much older, it continued to be difficult for me to be aware of the difference between the real happenings and the ones in my head. Some of the

people in those stories were more real to me than many of
the actual people I encountered. Reality, truth and scientific
fact are sometimes what we wish them to be: analogs of
fantasy.

As a boy, I especially enjoyed reading the Fables of La
Fontaine; Grimm's Tales; the Adventures of Baron
Munchausen; Don Quixote; Edgar Allan Poe's stories and
Rabelais' Gargantua and Pantagruel. In a way, these were
an introduction to my long lasting love for Fantasy and
Science Fiction, which covers every imaginable form of
literary expression from romance and adventure to social
and political satire — you see, not all Science Fiction
concerns itself with Star Wars and Bug Eyed Monsters from
Outer Space.

The Travelling Teller of Tales had his own Sci-fi stories.
When, for instance, he told of a Djinn hobgoblin who could
be freed by a human from the small bottle in which he was
trapped in order to fulfil that human's impossible wishes,
or when the Teller introduced into his narrative an
intelligent machine that could walk and talk and perform
amazingly powerful feats. . . when he described space
travellers who arrived from distant stars on magic flying
carpets guided by weird winged creatures he was, in fact,
re-telling legends which can be found in the ancient
mythologies of every culture in human history.

When, in describing the scenario for one of his tales, he
referred to a flood that buried the whole of our planet under
water, or to a massive explosion triggered off by one of the
Lords of the Skies that destroyed an entire continent, he
was telling tales that had been passed down by generations
of story tellers over many centuries — and many of these
tales had been woven into the religious beliefs, the histories
and the superstitions of all civilizations throughout the
history of conscious humankind. Some of the extraordinary

events may have actually occurred, and while scientists search eagerly for evidence' of such happenings in rocks and with extrapolations of weather patterns, science fiction writers continue to tell their tales of fantasy, which very occasionally develop into fact.

When the Travelling Teller of Tales wove into one of his tall stories the exotic customs of pygmies, of giants and of other strange peoples, he was easily able to convince us that such customs existed. In some cases, as I discovered many years later, what he had been telling us was the truth — exaggerated, distorted, rendered grotesque to suit his narrative, but still based on real facts. I can only guess that he may have obtained some of his information from old magazines — or he may by chance have come across an illustrated world encyclopedia, because at least a few of the strange things he described had their origins in the Amazon, the Pacific islands, Australasia or in the Far East.

All the same, that old itinerant had an untamed look of wanderlust about him, like those wiry ownerless dogs that roamed the barren outskirts of villages and towns, and there is little doubt that he had been up the Nile at least as far as the Sudan and probably well beyond. He had made his pilgrimage to Mecca, moved across the Gulf States, and then over the Red Sea to Persia. He had been to Baghdad, and he had talked about his encounters up north with the Turks and the Albanians. He almost certainly travelled west to Libya and Morocco and may well have crossed over to Gibraltar and then into Spain. He had travelled as far east as India by boat, working his free passage by entertaining the men below decks with his bawdy anecdotes. He could speak Swahili — that mixture of Bantu and Arabic which is the vernacular language of East Africa — and he imitated skilfully the wide variety of Arabic dialects spoken in the Middle East. It is difficult, for instance, for a Moroccan to

follow the colloquial Arabic spoken by a Kuwaiti, and it
might be necessary for them to converse in the literary
language of the Koran in order to understand each other.

*   *   *

One evening at dusk, rather later than his custom, the Teller
of Tales arrived looking careworn and dusty. There was an
unfamiliar vagueness about him, a desultory picking at the
food specially prepared for him by the women, a weary
response to Mabrooka's teasing. His mood of preoccupied
civility, his melancholy — we would have called it *angst* if
the word had been known to us — made it clear that we
were unlikely to be treated to any lighthearted tales about
Goha that evening.

He was not a young man, and in the oblique light of that
incandescent orange disc falling rapidly below the horizon,
the lines on his face were deepened in shadow so that his
skin seemed furrowed and parched like the neck of the
large tortoise in the nuns' convent garden. He was very
tired and now he seemed much older. His small hooded
eyes were set deep in the blue rims of their sockets and the
irises were ringed with opaque white circles. His eyesight
was obviously very poor because, in his upper coat pocket,
he carried a pair of antique spectacles with thick pebble
lenses which he used for reading, his nose no more that an
inch from the paper. Both his ghallabeya, with its ancient
broad leather belt on which his small money pouch was
attached, and his knee-length collarless dark coat had loose
threads where the edges were frayed. The sides of his
leather slippers had oval patches sewn on them with coarse
waxed thread and their small brass buckles were rough with
verdigris. Sitting beside him as we sipped our tea, I noticed,
for the first time, that the Teller's heels were ridged with

callouses which were deeply split and that his ankles and
calves were thin and slightly scaly with crackled powdery
skin. And that when he rose, his hand went to his back as
he tightened his lips with pain. He held out his other hand
as though requesting me to help him, but when I stood up
to do so, he put his hand to my head and whispered quietly:
"Rab'binna Khal'leek". Which means: 'God preserve you'.
Then he walked slowly toward his already seated audience,
lifting each foot high off the ground with every step. It
reminded me of the way camels ambled flat-footed across
the dunes without burying their feet in the soft sand.

Facing the semi-circle of eager faces and ready to tell his
tale, that exhausted old man gathered the necessary stamina
from some reservoir of strength deep within himself to put
on the show he could in no way allow himself to put off.
His eyes were now much larger, no longer dull but
glistening with energy. His turban was no longer straight
but set at a rakish angle over his forehead. He was standing
tall, as he always did when telling his tales. He no longer
looked old and feeble. He looked dangerous.

I discovered many years later that he was what, in the
English theatre, is called 'an old trouper' and that it is one
of the enduring theatrical clichés like 'the show must go
on'.

And so he drew back his elbows to flex his shoulder blades,
cracked his knuckles loudly and clapped his hands in
preparation for the bravura performance his audience had
paid for. Yes, ladies and gentlemen, you leave all your pain
and hurt and misery behind in the dressing room and you
go out there and give the best performance of your life. Ask
any old trouper.

*   *   *

It was many years ago — he began by telling us — that he
had encountered the pygmies who live in caves on the face
of a mountain precipice. It was with great fear in his heart
that he had undertaken the perilous journey to locate them
in order to obtain a rare medicine which only they knew
how to concoct. They were primitive savages he warned us
with great seriousness — as though we might be foolhardy
enough to rush off en masse and pay them a visit —
primitive savages who would kill any unwelcome intruder
with a single poison-tipped arrow from a blowpipe and then
punch a hole in his skull and suck his brain out with a
hollow bamboo. It was the smaller brains of women that
they found most delectable — a ghoulish aside to Mabrooka
which drew the desired shriek of alarm from her on cue.

He went on to explain that the Sultan of Yemen, no less,
had commissioned him to obtain a cure for the rapid waning
of the prowess with which Allah, in his munificence, had
endowed him for the purpose of enriching the world with
the issue from his loins. If such was the Will of Allah, how
could he, a humble Travelling Teller of Tales, have refused
to embark on such a noble quest. But he was distracting
us. . . surely we now wished him to regale us with Goha's
latest escapade. No? He should continue with the tale of
this astounding adventure? This mission of great secrecy
which he had never previously disclosed to anyone? We
wished him to betray a sacred confidence? So be it, he
conceded, but only, he added, because he knew that we
were a tribe whose honour was known far and wide as
being beyond question. I rejoiced inwardly at the thought
that I had been included in that tribute to such a worthy
tribe.

"Very well then" the Teller of Tales said patiently "let it be
known that in order to carry out my mission I had to
survive a perilous journey along dark tributaries of the Nile

which have remained undiscovered to this day by those
feverish and ill-tempered English explorers who roamed the
African continent in search of its source. We already know"
— he informed us with a sly wink — "that the source of
that holy river springs from the very lips of The Almighty
One. Ah, but let them search, let the fools explore! Allah
will surely swallow them in one gulp and then spit them
out for the wild beasts to feed on. For that is the just
avengement of the Almighty upon the intemperate curiosity
of those pale infidels!"

"Yes indeed" he went on, working up some agitated
fidgeting in his audience "and you would recognise these
foreign scavengers from their absurd appearance, even from
a great distance. They always wear pith helmets and white
tunics fitted with many pockets in which they keep their
pipes, their useless maps, compasses, bunches of keys, little
balls of string and liver pills. Tucked in the sleeve cuffs of
their tunics are the foul handkerchiefs with which they
constantly mop the sweat from their brows and into which
they blow the muck from their noses — much to the disgust
of the Nubian porters who discharge their nasal mucous to
the ground in a hygienic and respectable manner, just as we
all do"

"Ah yes" he continued in a more reflective tone "I met a
party of these stumbling curiosity seekers on that section
of my journey which traversed a deep jungle, and they
enquired of me if they had perchance, in my considered
opinion as a native of this vast continent, taken the wrong
turning some days before. You see my friends, they were
unaccustomed to finding their way around without the help
of street signs, as one sees in towns and cities. Taking pity
on the poor souls I gave them guidance on how to find their
way to the comforts of the nearest European hotel some
hundreds of leagues to the north. I relied, of course, on my

expert navigational gift in interpreting the position of the sun in the day and the configuration of the stars at night, a knowledge bestowed upon me by the Wazir of Astrology to the Bey of Tunis. I may inform you that it was my reward for saving his favourite catamite from drowning while frolicking in the palace fountains. This boy was gifted with great prettiness and exquisitely versed in the erotic art of. . . but forgive me for this unwelcome digression. . ."

He pursed his lips and glanced coyly at Lateef, that dainty nephew of Abu Bakr, who was a mild embarrassment to the community for his continued vociferous objections to marriage at the advanced age of thirty. Moreover, he had a penchant for singing the latest love ballads of Abdel Wahab and Om Kalsoom in his reedy voice and for dyeing the palms of his hands and soles of his feet with henna, like Mabrooka, with whom he would often share a giggling banter and gentle wrist slapping.

It was accepted that every community may be burdened with one of nature's misfits, unfortunates who should be treated with the respect due to any human being, and that it can consider itself fortunate if the poor wretch is not possessed of *affreets*, those evil spirits that cause their host to commit acts of obscenity or violence. Lateef was endowed with the slightly plump and beautiful curves that were the envy of many of the women, and the elegance of his gestures and general demeanour was such that the effeminate *affreet* who dwelt in him was to become, over the years, as much a tenant of the tribe as the spirits of manliness and courage with which the other men were imbued.

And now, seated on his little mat at the foot of the tall weather-beaten Teller of Tales, unwelcome attention had been drawn to Lateef — not cruelly, but with a kindly humour which, nonetheless, he had found painful. He had been rubbing his belly with unconscious zest in anticipation of the shocking particulars that might, with some luck, titillate those repressed emotions within him which had lain fallow, secretly and shamefully buried for so long. He grinned sheepishly — his disappointment betrayed by his downcast and rapidly blinking eyes — as he quickly drew the hem of his ghallabeya over his small bare feet with their long and delicate toes.

The Teller of Tales shook his head in a fleeting movement of remorse at having inadvertently caused discomfort to that innocent who had always been as entranced by his romantic tales as a bride-to-be, and also for having his well-intentioned jest greeted with silence by the rest of his audience. He clapped his hands together loudly to draw our attention away from that momentary lapse and continued as though there had been no interruption to his narrative: "I spent a day and a night with the Englishmen and observed with pity their insect-bitten white legs, red faces and tiny pink private parts which they did not bother to hide in shame when washing themselves with scented soap in the river, like the Khedive's playful concubines"

He drew closer to us and spoke barely audibly so that we had to dismiss the last remaining vestiges of awareness in our real surroundings in order to catch his faint words in the dim light of the paraffin lamps. In the distance a feral she-cat growled hideously in the spiky pain of copulation, a fortuitous sound effect which he managed to exploit with simulated wide-eyed alarm. With a trembling finger pointing toward the source of that sound, coming from quite nearby in the darkness surrounding us, he muttered hoarsely: "At sundown in that fearful jungle, with the cries of wild beasts no more than a few paces away, the Englishmen's tents were pitched with much fussing by them over the correct tension of ropes and straightness of poles.

Later, these men sat at folding tables with white linen cloths and ate the contents of tins of food served on plates decorated with pictures in a blue colour. Their silver knives and forks had ivory handles made from the tusks of the elephants they were wisely hoping to avoid meeting in the dark of night, for it is known that elephants have long memories and do not approve of such frivolous abuse of their magnificent tusks". He shook his head haughtily to show his own disapproval.

"For the rest of the evening, they drank large quantities of Scotch Whisky and sang merrily until they toppled over and had to be carried to their camp beds by the Nubian porters who mocked them loudly in their own tongue. *Ya din el Nabi!* when one thinks that it is Englishmen such as these who despoiled the tomb of our great King Tu Tankh Amoun!" he wailed, shaking his fist in outrage as though he had been appointed sole caretaker of the sacred sarcophagi and other treasures by the Pharaoh himself. And I was not embarrassed by these disclosures for the simple reason that I was never able to associate myself with the behaviour of most fair-skinned people, even when I grew to be an old man in the country of my paternal ancestors.

The Teller of Tales continued: "I finally reached a deep valley of perpetual rain in which the massive trees grew so close together that the thinnest man could barely pass between them. . . trees that towered above us twice as high as the tallest minarets of our Holy Mosque in the great Citadel in Cairo. In the very heart of that valley, rising high above me, I came to a vertical cliff face pierced by the mouths of caves that I knew must be the abode of the pygmy people"

He performed a pirouette as he shouted: "Suddenly I was surrounded by a group of thirty tiny men squealing like frantic children and pointing at me with awe. The biggest of them only reached up to my knee. They stood there gibbering and dancing up and down with excitement as though they had come face to face with a supernatural being. . . a divine creature springing to life miraculously out of their most powerful legend. Yes, my friends! For what else was it but my foresight in bedecking myself with a hundred small mirrors tied to my ghallabeya that convinced these small people that I was an incarnation of their ancestral Sun God! I stood glimmering and shimmering and sparkling in a misty shaft of sunlight which at that moment had pierced through the dense foliage above. Ah, my friends, such a bright beam may only rarely be seen by the devout when the Prophet's sword of light cuts through the darkness in the Holiest Place in Mecca at a time of prayer. So I addressed them thus. . ." — the Teller of Tales lowered his voice to a low-pitched sonorous tone with a contrived echo in the prolonged vowel sounds as he intoned: *"An-aaah Hin-aaaaaaah!"* — which simply means 'I am here' in Arabic.

After a pause in which he scanned his audience to ensure that he had their full attention, he continued in a casual explanatory way: "They did not understand our language of course, nor did I understand theirs. But no matter, for I was able to communicate with them in that occult universal sign language taught to me by the Grand Wazir of Morocco — the most Powerful Wazir of all — who can make fierce lions mew like kittens and who can order a swarm of locusts to fly out into the ocean and drown. It is a language understood by a few primitive aboriginals and by all animals and most birds — other than the Fiery Phoenix of Madagascar that can speak all human languages and therefore has no need of signs. This elusive bird — I am able to speak of it with some authority, having debated the relative efficiency of the varied mating habits of feathered creatures with one such Phoenix for a whole night — has wings tipped with the purest gold. These rare feathers, shed but once every ten years, are gathered and used to decorate the magnificent ceremonial garments worn by the Holy Alchemists of the Beneen people. . . a tribe of giants whose skills in the casting of heads in bronze had been passed on to them by visitors from another world. The alien creatures, with the bodies of men and heads of lizards, needed to repair the engine of their space chariot and it had come to pass, by good fortune, that they alighted out of the heavens in the country of the Beneen, who were unequalled in the craft of metal work. Ah, but I have foolishly strayed into another tale, have I not? No no, we must now return to the pygmies, the small people. . . is that not so?"

Bemused by the prospect of receiving two extraordinary tales instead of one — of pygmies *and* of giants — we hoped that he would, in some astonishing way, weave both tales into a single monumental saga. We started to protest. But it was enough for him that he had whetted our appetite for a forthcoming attraction, and so he patted the palms of his hands toward us in a quietening gesture and continued with his original tale.

"Well, my friends, the pygmies invited me to climb their network of rope ladders and swinging bridges, which were so cunningly woven that they easily supported my superior weight, and I finally reached their largest cave. This was the main chamber, a vast hole in the belly of the mountain, connected by many tunnels hewn out of the solid rock to all the dwelling caves. It is in that place that they performed all their secret ritual ceremonies and celebrated their triumphal feasts. For you see, in spite of their diminutive size, they were great warriors much feared by other tribesmen of normal dimensions. They killed, I discovered, neither for food nor for profit of any kind. They killed for pure pleasure. Is this not a noble thing my friends? Ah yes, but what, then, did they eat, you are asking yourselves? Let me tell you: they ate seeds as large as pomegranates and figs as small as raisins, and they drank an inebriating broth fermented from the crushed root of the poisonous yam which the women rendered harmless with their rancid spittle. It was enough to corrode your innards like the quicklime which burns all living flesh. The men smoked the aromatic leaves of the snake vine which turned them into snakes and they sniffed the spores of the frog mushroom and became frogs. And then they tied the ends of aerial roots, such as we find on our banyan trees, to their ankles and hurled themselves headfirst from the tops of the tallest trees, stopping only a hair's breadth from the ground below. This was their sport as well as their proof of fearless manhood"

"Ah, and why did they defy death in this foolhardy manner?" He purred the question at us and answered it in the same breath: "Listen, my friends, they did so because they had no fear of death, for it did not exist with them. When one of their people died, they merely placed the deceased one in a seat attached to the cliff-face and assumed that the person was still present though unwilling to participate in the activities of others. The humid atmosphere and the exotic concoctions which they consumed during life preserved them in much the same manner as the mummies of our ancient kings and queens. Naturally they did not look too attractive after a while, but the small people are not all that attractive to start with and so the difference was barely noticeable. They would often speak casually to the corpses, informing them of some rare event such as the birth of a live infant, or occasionally consult them for advice about the most auspicious time to plant their yams or to make a murderous raid on a village down the valley"

He lowered his voice almost to a whisper: "As for their appearance. . . it was stranger than anything you will ever see. The women inserted circular discs fashioned from thin slabs of mineral glass, which was plentiful in their mountain, into a slit cut in their lower lips. This, they deluded themselves into believing, made them more attractive. And as they grew older they would periodically insert larger discs until some were like big glazed portholes, such as we may see on passing ships, hanging down over their breasts"

Now he raised his voice: "Do I detect the shaking of heads in disbelief? No no no, my worthy friends, I tell but the truth. The Sheikh of Khartoum has his daily breakfast of honeyed dates served upon such a disc, which I received as a gift from the small people on my departure. Let me explain: the Sheikh had done me the generous favour of releasing me from the custody of his guards who had arrested me on a charge of practising the black art of necromancy. Such injustice! Why, I was only innocently affording pleasure in the serene privacy of the seraglio to a few of his younger wives with my flute. . . an instrument on which, in certain quarters, I am renowned for playing many a fine tune"

The Teller challenged us to think otherwise, with his eyebrows raised in a look of mock primness : "No, it was a trumped up charge, you must understand, brought against me by the older wives who had not benefited from the delights of my music"

He raised an eyebrow and gave a suggestive cough: "Ah, but the wise Sheikh, knowing the wily ways of women, expressed his sorrow over my plight: he granted me freedom on condition that I give him some rare artifact which might arouse the envy of that tiresome Sheikh of Aqa'ba who was always gloating about the collection of pickled human privy parts preserved in jars that he had bought from a Lebanese merchant. That most precious pygmy lip disc was the price for my liberty, my friends, otherwise I would have been able to produce that very object for you to examine as evidence of the veracity of my tale. . . alas, a tale from whose straight woven thread I stray once again. Forgive me, but I have travelled in the heat of the summer sun for many hours so that I may reach you before sundown, and my thoughts are wandering for want of a sip of your invigorating tea"

That was the signal for the interval — the universal break in every theatrical performance that enables the audience to stretch its stiffened legs, to attend to the call of nature and to slake its thirst.

After the Teller of Tales and the other men had withdrawn for a short while into the darkness and returned, nonchalantly scratching their groins, to take their tea — which had been brewed by boiling the tea-leaves until they were pale grey, all the caffeine and tannin having been leached out, and the black liquid poured into a glass half filled with sugar — the tale resumed: "Allahhhh. . . my noble friends, that was most refreshing. Allow me now to tell you that the pygmy men drink a tea infused from the leaves of a rare eucalypt. It has the remarkable property of enabling them to go without sleep for a whole month. Indeed, it was the great Kemal Al Turki himself who begged me to hand over the supply I had brought back with me so that his courageous border guards would remain alert in their constant vigil against savage attack by the predatory and treacherous Greeks. How could I refuse such a worthy request?" He raised his hands skyward in supplication.

"But to continue: the pygmy men would spend many hours of the day decorating their whole bodies in strange patterns with pale coloured earth pigments that they had mixed into a paste with their urine. They also wore long conical sheaths, made from the leaves of the banana tree, over their disproportionately large penises which they kept in a vertical position with plaited thongs made from the hair plucked from the heads of. . ."

He was interrupted by a loud spluttering noise as Mabrooka choked on her pink sherbet drink. A frothy spray spurted into the air from her nostrils, followed by a fit of coughing punctuated by her confused cries of: "I am dead! I am dying!" Lateef, with an expression of panic distorting his chubby face, held her hand and patted her back helplessly.

This brought the Teller of Tales to a frozen standstill. He seemed in a trance which continued well after Mabrooka had recovered. It was, you will have guessed, that moment of terror with which even the most experienced actors in the theatre are sometimes afflicted. They dry up. They have forgotten their lines. They may well have forgotten which play they are supposed to be acting in, what theatre, indeed, what town they are in. The sympathetic efforts of the other actors on stage to prompt them back into the scenario may only make things worse. The sudden amnesia drives them into making feeble gestures and muttering meaningless phrases while they desperately grope for the path back to the reality — or measured unreality — of their performance. It has been said that some of the great playwrights' finest dialogue was improvised on the spur of the moment by actors who dried up on stage. Well, perhaps.

We did our best to prompt him by calling out key words such as 'pygmies' and 'penises' and 'urine' to the poor man who now appeared to have been deprived of the climactic moment he had so painstakingly worked up to. We were only making matters worse, because he made no response, remaining perfectly still and expressionless. We gradually fell into an anxious silence, waiting for him to recover his memory.

Suddenly he became animated, rapidly shuffling his feet in a mad ritual dance, waving his arms above his head and spinning round wildly, like the troupe of Darweesh who had once performed their dances for us at the end of Ramadan. The Teller of Tales then stopped abruptly, confronting us in the cloud of dust he had raised. "Pygmies? Penises?" he enquired with a breathless ferociousness as he pointed to the ground with his forefingers. Still gasping for breath and with droplets of sweat flicking off his face he roared: "What are these but shifting dust risen from the earth? And such as we shall all be in the end? It is the will of Allah! Yes, worthy friends, and it was no less the Will of Allah that I return at once to the Sultan of Yemen with my mission accomplished"

As we sat in a state of shock, he stalked off beyond the irregular ring of light cast by the paraffin lamps. He had disappeared offstage, into the wings, as actors and ballet dancers sometimes do after a stunning tour de force, only to return in order to acknowledge the applause of an entranced audience.

He had squatted some distance away on his haunches, in the dark blue shadow of Ibn Mahmood's small brick hut that was silhouetted against the moonlight. We clapped our hands and called out to him loudly, we begged him to come back and finish his tale. He rose slowly, returning in a brisk waddle to the primitive spotlights where he bowed low while making the solemn deferential gesture of touching his brow and then his lips with the tips of his fingers before his hands came to rest by his side, palms facing upwards. He got his round of applause.

"Thank you greatly — *met'shakkir jiddan* — honourable
Badaoui people. Allow me, then, to come to the end of my
astounding tale. The magical concoction was extracted by
the pygmies from the gonads of captured apes who spend
their entire lives on top of the canopy formed by the tall
jungle trees. No, the agile beasts never descend to the
ground, for they live off the limitless supply of moist young
leaves and berries and insects found at that level. And so,
spared from the burden of hunting for food, they occupy
their time with incessant copulation, day and night, night
and day, hour upon hour. Upon my word, the mightiest trees
quake beneath their ardent romping. Locked in ecstatic
embraces, they leap from branch to branch and bounce this
way and that"

He jumped up and down, at the same time rotated his hips
in a grotesque parody of the apes' frantic coupling.
Stopping in a cloud of dust, and gasping for breath after
that stunning acrobatic demonstration, he panted:

"Yes. . . aaaah. . . huhhh. . . yes. . . aaaah. . . huhhh. . .
the male apes have thus become endowed with formidable
organs for that purpose! Yes indeed. And it is from those
very organs, dried and ground to the finest powder and
mixed with the juices crushed from the cantharides fly that
the precious elixir is concocted. I gave the small people my
mirrors in return for their kindness and generosity and
departed, leaving them staring at their reflections and
believing that their numbers had thus been magically
increased a hundredfold"

It was all too much for Mabrooka's comprehension. She
interrupted him with a peevish snort, calling out loudly:
"What were you doing dancing about like that you old
camel? What is all this nonsense you are telling us?"

The Teller of Tales looked at her with exaggerated
amusement. This hostile heckling was something that every

seasoned performer has had to deal with at some time or other, and he was ready for it. Unflustered by Mabrooka's antics — she was now standing and cackling at the rest of us like an ancient hen that has laid an unexpected egg and is scratching the earth around it in celebration — he answered her with excessive politeness: "Oh gracious madam, with your generous permission I shall reach the end of my journey without further ado and I therefore humbly beg you to. . ."

"Well get on with it" she screeched at him "otherwise we shall reach your destination before you do. Just get on with it, you old fool!"

We were spellbound by this impromptu badinage, some of us even believing that it may have been previously rehearsed by the Teller of Tales, using Mabrooka as a counterpoint to the smooth progress of his tale in order to keep us on tenterhooks.

The old man continued: "I left the pygmy people with the priceless concoction for the Sultan of Yemen locked in my satchel. I knew it to be safe in that repository, which was made from the impenetrable hide of a bull crocodile captured on the reed banks of the Upper Nile by the strangest of all primitive peoples: the purple-skinned M'bongwato tribe. Ah, hear this, noble friends, hear this: it is their womenfolk who are the warriors and hunters. They fit bronze rings round their necks and they keep adding more rings as their necks stretch, until their heads tower no less than ten hands above their shoulders. They are a truly fearsome sight as they utter menacing cries from their lengthened voice pipes and brandish their spears threateningly at those who trespass upon their territory. As for the men: they spend all their time grooming themselves prettily, gossiping, and wearing flowers behind their ears while cooking dainty dishes and singing and caring for their

children. Is this not truly an abomination against the laws
of nature, as decreed by the Holy Prophet Mohammad
himself! Oh Allah The Mightiest, but what shall be shall
be. So be it"

That last piece of information drew gasps of incredulity
from most of the older members of the audience with the
exception of Mabrooka, who let out a screech of scornful
laughter and squawked: "Then their men are a lot more
useful than you, you ridiculous old goat"

"So be it" the Teller of Tales repeated a little tetchily in her
direction. The smirking boss-eyed woman was cocking one
impertinent eye at him, while the other seemed to be
scanning some of the family within its orbit with a glint of
defiance. Levelling his firm gaze at the sprightly old
woman he boomed: "Now hear this: I travelled to the land
of the Ethiopians, where I entertained the Greatest of All
Emperors, The Most Magnificent Hayee El Selassee with
my best tales of Goha. It was he, my friends, who granted
me the title of Teller of Tales To The Golden Throne. From
thence I journeyed across the sea by dhow to the Yemen.
And so to. . ."

"Get on with it, you old fool!" Mabrooka repeated

"My sweetheart — *Ya habibtee*" the Teller of Tales replied
tartly, throwing his arms out as though to embrace
Mabrooka from a safe distance, "in your haste to rush to
the end of my adventure before I do, is it conceivable that
you may not have heard that, precisely nine months after
my arrival, thirty-three of the Sultan of Yemen's wives had
all borne him sons, and all on the very same day?"

He had not let us down. We had been under his control all
along — and he had led us to believe, there, for a while,
that he was losing his touch. How very clever of him! What
extraordinary adventures he must have had in all his

travels! We could never hope to experience such things —
not even if we lived to be as old as he. No, he was no mere
teller of tales. He was more, so much more.

He received a good long round of applause and much
laughter, and none more enthusiastically than from a
fair-haired blue-eyed little boy, who was so bewitched and
inspired by the old man's fantasies that his greatest wish
was to be able to tell such tales when he grew old and
experienced and wise like The Travelling Teller of Tales.

The Businessman

Before he became a teacher of English at a small private
school in Alexandria, my father had been in business for
some years as an importer and sole distributor in Egypt for
Lawrence Leathers Company Inc. and for Robbie Burns
Scotch Whisky. He had, at some stage, trustingly but
unwisely supplied a charming and plausible Hungarian
rogue called Erno Bortoli with a very large consignment of
cases of that whisky. Bortoli had rapidly sold almost the
entire stock at an unprofitable discount to a number of bars
and hotels in Cairo. He had followed the scam with a
conspicuous spending spree on the proceeds — his
self-confident ebullience greatly bolstered by a continuous
and heavy daily sampling of some of the heady liquor that
he had, with foresight, reserved for his own consumption.

The man and the money were fairly rapidly exhausted as
he satisfied his insatiable appetite for expensive food and
appreciably more expensive women, both of which he was
more often than not inclined to indulge in at the same time
— as the various madames and restaurateurs attested at his
brief trial before the Crimes Tribunal in Cairo. He ended
up serving a short prison sentence. My father went out of
business, and that should have been that, as far as he was
concerned, because he was temperamentally incapable of
bearing a grudge. Besides, as he remarked on more than
one occasion to my mother, it had surely been made all too
easy for Bortoli to commit the crime. Should the criminal

bear the full burden of his crime, my father pondered aloud over a cup of tea, or was it partly the fault of his own ineptitude in placing temptation in the path of a man who may otherwise have been law-abiding? Should he himself, my father reasoned, not share a measure of guilt for that error of judgement? Pay some small price for his failure to anticipate the likelihood of wrongdoing? Was he not an indirect participator in the commissioning of a crime and therefore deserving of some retribution from the Almighty? He looked pale and weary.

While he had worthily agonized for a long period over the profound moral, religious, and philosophical implications of the disastrous episode that had left him penniless and humiliatingly reduced to soliciting small sums of money periodically from his widowed mother in order to buy food for us. . . my mother had understandably adopted a somewhat different attitude. She refused to make any allowances at all for Bortoli. The man was a criminal who had robbed us of the very food from our mouths.

"How," she wondered with amazement, "could you be so weak as to make excuses for this repugnant specimen of humanity? — no, it is odious of that ogre to have committed such an act of betrayal after having been trusted. . . after breaking bread in our own home and after having my child on his knee. . . and he even stroked the boy's head! It is obscenely hypocritical. That despicable man has placed our child's very life at hazard by his treacherous conduct in robbing our family. I hate him, yes I truly hate him and wish him dead."

Seeing the shocked expression on my father's face, she added: "And if sacred hatred is a sin against your God, then He can peddle His notion of sin elsewhere for all I care"

I could sense that my mother and father were unlikely ever to reach agreement on this issue. After a while my father got a job teaching English at the school and they both stopped making any reference to Bortoli.

My father, as it happens, did not receive his salary from his employer for several months, during which time we continued to subsist on my grandmother's meagre subventions, which was as much as she could spare. Nor had Mahroos received any wages for a long time, yet neither he nor my father seemed to be all that outwardly troubled — in spite of my mother's protests — by the fact that they were not being paid for their work.

Now, there was that unfamiliar word my mother had used. It had caught my attention and it had lingered in my mind. It was the word *hate*. I wondered, then, what it felt like to hate someone. I still don't know precisely what it feels like, but perhaps I know the reason *why* I don't. And no, I don't believe that this necessarily means that I am nice person. . . I simply think that I may not have inherited the gene marked *hate*. Perhaps it's a weakness, a defect. Like being tone deaf or colour blind. Or could it be a cautious resistance to fear — the ancestor of hatred? During a war, everyone is called upon to hate the enemy, but the men who are given weapons and ordered to go out and kill that enemy never hate him as such — not unless these men are fanatical maniacs. In battle there is no room for hatred, it's a fearful and immediate question of survival. I remember who was 'hated' during the war: it was the politicians and the generals who sent us off to kill and possibly to die, often uselessly, while they waited in safety for statistics about the numbers slaughtered in the macabre games they played with human lives.

Over the years I gave a lot of thought to the meaning of hatred, of fear, and of anger and I came to the conclusion that they meant pretty much the same thing — they are simply variations of the response to a threat to our instinct for survival. The instinct for survival is what determines all our actions. . . everything we do, even our slightest gestures can be traced back in a straight line to that unique inheritance.

*   *   *

Some time after the Bortoli incident and following my mother's not unreasonable insistence that my father should make some attempt to recover the money owed to him by his other erstwhile customers, my father nervously set off to pay a visit to Monsieur Maxim Bakhramian, a pillar of the local Armenian community. He took me with him, probably because he needed the supportive company of an unquestioning and uncritical human being on a difficult mission such as this.

Maxim Bakhramian was a manufacturer and importer of children's toys — among a number of his other businesses, which included property development and some entrepreneurial activities that my mother had described as 'louche' . He had, over the years, ordered and obtained several consignments of expensive calf and patent leather hides from my father, none of which he had paid for. His office and warehouse were in the centre of the town.

As soon as we arrived the man greeted my father with the demonstrative welcome given to a much loved brother who had been presumed lost at sea and miraculously come back to life. He then picked me up and kissed the top of my head, put me down and, with an affectionate pat on the backside, directed me toward rows of shelving packed with every imaginable kind of toy.

As I rummaged in a trance of wonderment in that Aladdin's cave of children's games, dolls, toy soldiers, model cars and tractors and fire-engines and other clockwork treasures, I could hear my father in the office reasoning with Bakhramian. I was disturbed to hear a pleading tone in my father's voice. . . it was undignified, and worse, I could sense that he was struggling with the humiliation that he was experiencing. I could not hear all the words being spoken, but Bakhramian was making angry grunting sounds. . . and there was a tone of finality in his responses as he raised his voice with impatience at my father's persistent requests for settlement of the debt. I could no longer play with the toys and so I sat on the dusty floor staring at the open office doorway and waiting anxiously for the dreadful confrontation to come to an end.

Finally they both appeared, with Bakhramian's hand resting heavily on my father's back in a gesture of amicable forbearance and, at the same time, guiding him firmly to the door leading out into the street. My father was stooped in defeat and was clearly distressed. As I ran toward them, Bakhramian reached out and picked a cuddly toy lamb made from real lamb's-wool off a nearby shelf and handed it to me with a benign smile and then turned to my father and said grimly: "You should have taken greater care in running your business, Louis, and now you expect me to throw good money after bad. Go home and look after your family and do not waste my time again"

We were walking along the busy street on our way to the tram terminal when a young beggar approached us holding out his hand for alms. As my father reached in his pocket for a coin, I impulsively handed the beggar the toy lamb. It was not a charitable act — the truth of the matter is that here, by some stroke of fortune, was a perfect excuse to get rid of the beastly thing. Frightened and confused, he handed it over to my father, who, puzzled by my unseemly gesture, returned it to me. I thrust it back in the beggar's hands and

ran down the road, as though pursued by the shame and
anger I had felt outside Bakhramian's office. My father
soon caught up with me and, in one swift movement, lifted
me on to his shoulders and walked on with his body erect,
gripping my ankles protectively.

The Chameleon

I had a favourite chameleon that lived among the variegated ficus shrubs. It would stand quite still with its long prehensile fingers and toes gripping the thin bough on which it was poised, its bulging eyes rotating independently while scanning for prey. Eventually a moth or a cricket would venture within striking distance. The chameleon would move in slow motion toward its intended meal and, having judged the distance accurately, it would uncoil its tongue and strike with amazing rapidity. The chameleon's tongue is almost as long as its body and it has a sticky tip that glues itself to the insect before reeling it into the reptile's open jaws. But what impressed me even more was the chameleon's ability to camouflage its body to blend perfectly with the pattern of the background. Geckos could walk across ceilings, held there by the suction pads on their feet, and they could make loud screeching sounds in the night, but chameleons, I decided, were much more interesting — especially when they crawled slowly across your ghallabeya and gradually matched its pale colour.

I once invited Tonton to my secret retreat to observe the chameleon. The man had winced and only reluctantly accompanied me into the shrubbery, but once in the presence of the small reptile that looked like a miniature dinosaur, he had remained still and silent for a long time, mesmerized by its alertness and menacing patience.

Antoine Raphael Hettena must have been in his early
thirties when I saw him for the first time. It had been on
that special occasion when my mother had taken me along
to one of Madame Colombine Tabouret's famous al fresco
luncheon parties, where the charcoal broiled quail, red
mullet and lamb kebabs were judged as non pareil by eager
gourmets.

My mother had met Tonton, as everyone called him
affectionately, at Countess Zinnia's home. He was a
hairdresser by profession and was summoned regularly by
the Countess to shave her pubic hair as well as the hair
under her arms in the privacy of her boudoir. She had once
explained to my mother — while I pretended to be out of
earshot admiring her late husband's collection of erotic
bibelots in the corner vitrine — that there were three
perfectly good reasons for getting that engaging *farceur* to
perform the task: firstly, that she abhorred all body hair and
failed to appreciate why the Almighty, with infinitely
masculine wisdom, had inflicted that indignity upon
womankind; secondly, that she had a terror of accidentally
mutilating herself — *la peur bleue d'une malheureuse
circoncision, tu comprends Margot* — and thirdly, that
Tonton was both a deft artist with the cut-throat razor and
a discreet little *empapaouté, si j'ose dire*, she had added
with a confiding nod.

Madame Tabouret was an elderly, very thin and
frail-looking wealthy widow with an over-abundance of
volatile energy that severely debilitated anyone exposed to
prolonged contact with her. She lived alone — apart from
the cook, the housemaid, two decrepit dogs with chronic
eye infections and a savage Siamese cat — in a large top
floor apartment on the outskirts of the town, just one tram
stop away from the main terminus.

There was an exterior cast-iron staircase that led from her
kitchen to a large roof garden that she had furnished with
cane furniture and striped beach umbrellas, and that she had
filled with a dense undergrowth of potted flowering plants,
succulents and shrubs, as well as a few sizable fruiting
trees. It created the illusion of a rectangular section neatly
cut out of an exotic botanical garden and magically
transported to her rooftop. There were also strange
sculptures standing on marble plinths among the shrubs.
One, I recall, was a bird-like phallic totem with a mosaic
surface composed of sea-shells and fragments of porcelain
and coloured glass. It was my second favourite piece after
the imposing polished bronze phallus among the
hydrangeas. The mottled green serpentine marble phallus
by the rubber plant I found amusing, but it had somehow
failed to impress me.

Madame Tabouret employed an elderly Indian gardener to
tend her *jardin d'éden céleste*, as she called it, and it was
there that she presided over the gatherings of her flock of
artists, poets, intellectuals and dedicated eccentrics. She
rejoiced in their company and her close association with
them must have given her the feeling that she was, in some
wonderfully privileged way, sharing in the mystical talents
with which they had been uniquely endowed by a Superior
Being. They were exceptional individuals. . . and very
différent, après tout. . . which was further evidence of their
sublime rarity as far as she was concerned. She delighted
in showing them off to her wealthy friends in whose homes
she organized special soirées where the affluent bourgeoisie
and members of the foreign diplomatic services could rub
elbows safely and amusingly with her bohemian circus
without feeling socially compromised.

In return for her patronage, which also meant regular
financial contributions to their upkeep, her slightly freakish

gifted entourage performed their roles for her friends and their guests. They also frequently offered her gifts of some of their creative output, which she accepted with ceremonial cries of astonishment, obvious delight and much dabbing of tears of gratitude. There were enigmatic poems dedicated to her perceptive generosity that were read out in a dramatic monotone by the authors; tuneless lyrical songs in which she was likened to some legendary Greek goddess and which she was exhorted to sing in her cracked mezzo-soprano accompanied on the mandolin by the composer himself; painted portraits of her dressed in exotic costumes — I recall a large oil painting hanging in her 'studio' in which she was portrayed as a triumphant Joan of Arc in a shapely suit of armour, with her pet bulldogs Abelard and Héloïse by her side. There was another remarkable portrait in which she was Queen Cleopatra reclining seductively on a Louis XVI chaise-longue, surrounded by her little group of admirers dressed as pharaonic attendants. Tonton was portrayed as a puckish Mark Antony, standing behind her with one hand on his hip and the other expertly running a comb through her pageboy hairstyle.

But how did Tonton fit into their unconventional milieu? What exactly was his role? The simple truth is that he was probably lonely and had dovetailed himself smoothly into the group until such time as he could move on to something better suited to his restless and ambitious nature. They had welcomed him and had treated him as one of their own, a waif, an outcast in a world that failed to understand true aesthetic values. He was pale and plump and had clearly gone to great pains to model himself on Oscar Wilde's appearance, which he would presumably have obtained from photographs. But never having met the incomparable Oscar — who in any event had died when Tonton was a baby — he must have had some difficulty in emulating the writer's mannerisms and affected mode of speech. Yet beneath his mincing and effete exterior Tonton was resourceful and patiently determined to succeed.

True, he had perhaps gone a little over the top with the hip-rolling prancing and the disjointed wrist-flapping gestures, not to mention the lisping, the high-pitched giggles and the sulky pouting that made everyone laugh, if a little uneasily at times. But I could not help being moved by the heavenward rolling of the eyes that accompanied Tonton's deep sighs whenever he mentioned the little Bedouin boys who, he would remark wistfully, could look so much more *présentable* if they were not snotty and covered in grime and if their revolting ghallabeyas were occasionally laundered. I managed to relate a little self-consciously to that observation.

My mother was very fond of Tonton and never had any doubt that his heart was, in spite of his atrociously 'camp' buffoonery, firmly in the right place — *il a très bon coeur après tout*, my mother was constantly reminding my father, who was invariably polite to Tonton though he found the man's ambiguous affectation somewhat unnerving.

With his long boyish hair with its centre parting; his crumpled black velvet jacket; his lace-edged shirt and polka-dotted oversize silk cravat; the patent leather pumps encasing his tiny feet, and on his left index finger, the broad gold ring with its large lapis lazuli cabochon, Tonton Raphael Hettena had succeeded in creating a passable parody of Oscar Wilde for a look-alike contest. He may not have seen it in quite that way.

On the other hand, he would have been perfectly well aware of the outrageous picture he presented to others: after all, wasn't this perfectly fashioned persona grata his very own creative contribution to the world of art? Could he not be

seen as a fully three-dimensional living caricature —
ludicrous and misbegotten perhaps, but still a genuine
performing *objet d'art?* Was he not an accomplished
raconteur, delivering his carefully rehearsed epigrams off
the cuff, which, if they received a favourable response from
the listener, could be transformed into profound aphorisms
and later expanded into allegorical anecdotes that might
hold his captive audience spellbound as he cut, permed,
marcel waved, or uncrinkled their hair, or even shaved it,
as the case may be? He could see himself as a craftsman,
every bit as skilled as all the other mountebanks in the
group, and by far superior in one exceptional and dramatic
way. . .

He had, for some years, steeped himself in the fathomless
hot springs of the arcane sciences of psychology,
parapsychology and astrology. He read everything he could
lay his hands on about mesmerism and the ancient art of
hypnotism and read the novel Trilby. It had all been, he
confessed, *une véritable révélation.* He examined charts
that showed the functions of the various parts of the human
brain and read an article about phrenology in a magazine.
There was, therefore, little he did not know of the
functioning of the mind in relation to the important areas
of the brain and to the configuration of the cranium. He
finally came to realize that the power of the mind was
greater than anything else in the universe, and he also
discovered certain useful information about the Third Eye,
the I Ching, the Black Arts, Vampirism, the Spirit World,
Rosicrucians, Buddhism, Shamanism and a little about
curative herbs. The librarian at the Italian Hospital allowed
Tonton access to a copy of Gray's Anatomy, following his
assurance that his interest was purely scientific and neither
morbid nor prurient, and he was thus able to familiarize
himself with the general appearance of the human vascular

and nervous systems; the wide variety of organs; the musculature and skeletal structures, and a bit about embryology. At the same time, some of his earlier misconceptions regarding both male and female organs of generation were corrected and he was able, too, to memorize the Latin names of some of the more significant parts of the human anatomy. All this he revealed with uncharacteristic calm composure to my mother one afternoon at the villa.

How do I remember all this in such detail? One may *well* ask, because I frankly cannot recall all that clearly a conversation I had with a friend of mine only last week. . . all I can vaguely remember is that the discussion may have been meaningful, but that is only because my friend tends to take everything rather seriously. The workings of the mind and memory, as Tonton would undoubtedly have confirmed, are not all that easy to understand.

The turning point in his studies of the mind came suddenly one day when he came across an article about Sigmund Freud, the discoverer of psychoanalysis. At that very instant, Tonton told my mother, his life had been miraculously transformed. He knew at once that all the knowledge he had accumulated, indeed his very existence up to that time, had been a preparation, a vital prelude to the vocation that Destiny had chosen for him to follow.

With mounting excitement, and momentarily shedding his habitual lisp and languid grimaces, he described Freud's awe-inspiring insight in the case of an eighteen year old patient 'Dora' who had been afflicted by tragically conflicting sexual inclinations. Tonton described Freud's sessions with Dora as vividly as though he not only witnessed, but participated actively in the great man's analysis of her apparently intractable problem. It transpired that Dora's parents were very friendly with a Mr and Mrs 'K'.

Dora's father had a chest complaint and was being nursed by Mrs K with whom he was having an affair, which, as Freud uncannily detected, Dora seemed to be rather upset about. Mr K, meanwhile, showered Dora with gifts and made certain propositions to her. Dora was repelled by his advances and told her mother, whose reactions were not recorded. Although Freud never met Dora's mother, he dismissed the woman's relevance and wisely commented that she must by all accounts have been 'an uncultivated woman and above all a foolish one' who was only interested in domestic routine — a condition brilliantly diagnosed by him as *'housewife's psychosis'*.

It became clear to Freud, with his deep perception, that Dora was repressing her love for Mr K in spite of her revulsion toward him. So Freud informed her of her ambivalent feelings for Mr K, and disclosed to her the astonishing fact that the intensity of her love for her father led to her deep-rooted resentment of his affair with Mrs K. It is regrettable that it never became known if Dora's classic symptoms of *petite hysterie* — in short: her nervous cough, periodic loss of voice, occasional depression and unsociability together with what may have been periodic migraine — were successfully treated because she ended the treatment after three months. Freud expressed his grave disappointment, some years later, that he had not had the opportunity to advise Dora of her latent homosexual love for Mrs K, because it would undoubtedly have helped her to feel better about the whole lamentable situation.

Nevertheless, this was one of the six major cases upon which the foundation stone of psychoanalysis was laid, and it had proved beyond any shadow of doubt to Tonton that here, at last, was the key to the understanding and cure of all the ills of the mind. He went on to explain to my mother about an extraordinary genius called Gurdjieff who taught that we are all *'asleep'* and that we can free our *'true wills'* by understanding that we have *'three brains'* which govern our activity and our consciousness, and also by actively developing our self-awareness. And now — Tonton declared with the rapture of one who has seen the light — he was at last ready to fuse his accumulated knowledge into a process of true healing through scientific and spiritual enlightenment.

The last time I saw Tonton was about a year later when he called at our villa to pay his respects to my mother and to leave his visiting card. He had lost weight, his hair was trimmed *en brosse*, and he was wearing a well-tailored white sharkskin suit; a white silk shirt with wing collar and dark grey bow tie; a panama hat, and white high-button shoes with spats. He said very little on that final occasion and I was struck by the fact that his lisp and all the other mannerisms had been replaced by what I came to recognise many years later in others of his profession as 'genuine sincerity'. As he was getting into his new white Packard limousine, he turned round with a half apologetic smile and said: "I earned it, believe me. And it took a great deal of patience. Au revoir, mes chers amis". My mother must have been impressed by Tonton's extraordinary transformation because I found his visiting card fifty years later in a box among her old song sheets and photographs.

Docteur Antoine R. Hettena.
Diplôme. Vienne.

Conseilleur : Soins Spiritueuz.
Psychologue : Analyse Thérapeutique

Premier Étage. 32 Rue El Taher Pasha. Alexandrie.
Numéro Téléphonique: 623

Tonton may have got things just about right in fulfilling his
well-intentioned ambition to follow in the footsteps of the
great mystificators of his time — forerunners of the present
generation of manipulative therapist-gurus who combine
dubious techniques of psychoanalysis with the seductive
Eastern mystique of spiritual self-fulfilment in order to
captivate the spirit. It is actually self-surrender that these
practitioners demand of others and, in the process, they
create a dependency in which transference of feelings into
the relationship becomes an addiction, a monomania from
which there may be no satisfactory release for the seekers
after solace. That has also been an essential factor in the
foundation of great religions. It is the oldest story in the
world.

The Dictators

I sometimes overheard my parents and their friends discussing world events and world leaders.

There was Benito Mussolini whom the Italians called Il Duce, and whom everyone else thought was an ill-bred womanising political parvenu who had somehow risen from nothing to become Italy's dictator. Goodness only knows how he had managed it. Well, of course, he had all those hooligans, his Black Shirt Brigade, supporting him and they went around killing anyone who dared to disagree with him. And he was also making life *bien difficile* for that harmless little King Victor Emmanuel, who, in spite of the fact that he wore those high-heeled shoes because he was so short, was a gentleman. It must be intolerably embarrassing for *ce p'tit bonhomme* because that *gros plein de soupe* Mussolini was certainly *not* a gentleman. Just look at the arrogant way the man stuck out his big jaw and curled up his lower lip and made those awful speeches about how he was going to change Italy and then the whole world. Well, could you see a *cracheur* like him ruling the world in that preposterous little hat he wears? *Ma foie*, he looks more like one of the fat pageboys at the Excelsior. Oh yes, he'd sent his air force to bomb those wretched Abyssinians, and Mario at Groppi's was saying how the Italian soldiers chopped off the *macaronis* of their prisoners — or was it the other way round?

Anyway, it was barbaric and made everyone very nervous
and apprehensive about what Mussolini was going to do
next. There was no doubt he had his eye on the Sudan. And
that young King Farouk sending the Duce those obsequious
telegrams of congratulation just to keep on the right side of
him. . . *c'est ignoble!* The British Ambassador was keeping
his eye on Farouk, thank goodness, because he knew the
little *caneur* couldn't be trusted.

Of course Farouk's having an affair with Clarissa Chapman,
you know, young Julian Chapman's wife, yes Chapman
from the Consulate. Julian doesn't seem to mind. Well, he
was at Oxford, and he's a bit *fagot*, most of them *are* you
know. They say he only married old Wilfred Harrington's
daughter for the money so you can't blame the wretched
girl for her bit of *tromperie* on the side. Chapman's
superior, Basil Harlock, is not too happy about the whole
thing and he'd be a fool if he doesn't send Chapman back
home on the next boat. Doctor Berri at the Italian Hospital
is telling everyone that Farouk's got another dose of *chaude
pisse* — so goodness knows who else has caught it from *ce
petit cochon* by now.

One has to admit, though, that Mussolini has worked
wonders with the Italian economy. And look at all those
fine buildings he's putting up all over the place. Had
anyone seen the Railway Station in Milan? No? Well there
are those excellent photographs in the Illustrated London
News and one had to admit the railway station was
magnificent, with those massive sculptures and marble
columns — it reminded one of ancient Rome and the
Parthenon. *Oui, bien entendu,* the Parthenon was in Greece
but that doesn't make any difference, does it?

Anyway, the Duce was doing a lot more for his country
than that *petit salaud* of a dictator, Franco, whom the
Spanish called El Caudillo, and who was responsible for

that quite unnecessary civil war in which Bulkeley's son Kenneth was killed. We all told the little idiot he was quite mad to join the International Brigade. *C'est vraiment tragique.* What with that, and his poor mother Davina committing suicide she was so upset about the boy, no wonder Bulkeley went off his rocker and took to drink after losing lost his captaincy of the polo team at the Gezira Sporting Club.

Besides, what had Franco achieved for Spain? Let's make no mistake about it, if there *was* going to be another world war, that's if one paid any attention to all the warmongers, then El Caudillo was definitely going to have to take sides this time — he couldn't go on taking the coward's way out and remain neutral. Well, no, the Swiss had *always* been neutral, so it was quite different. Even old Señor Ramon, the head waiter back at the Yacht Club, had admitted he couldn't see Franco as a World Ruler: he conceded, a little ungraciously of course, that the man looks far too ludicrous in that silly little hat of his.

As for the Russians and their Communism, well it simply couldn't work, could it. Communal ownership of *everything*? It was beyond reason. *Absolument fada.* And that brute Stalin — he's a worse *fanatique* than *Raspoutine* — well he said in one of his speeches recently that within the next twenty years the whole world would turn to Communism because the workers would not put up with Capitalism for very much longer. Well of course that kind of propaganda is strictly for national consumption. *Voyons donc,* can you imagine the whole world eagerly turning to Communism? And the likes of that crabby old *fripouillard* Calouste Gulbenkian saying 'I don't need all this wealth, take it away from me, *je vous en supplie*? And Mr Joseph Stalin who, by this time has become Ruler of the World, says *'O! Merci beaucoup, monsieur!'* and then sends the *vieux couillon* off to Siberia to work in the salt mines! *Merde alors*, these madmen want to rule the whole world and that crafty *canaille* Stalin is no exception. Well, you wait, the Russian people will soon get wise to him and he'll be *foutu a la porte*. All that theoretical stuff that *bourrique* Karl Marx put into the heads of Lenin and his gang, well it's about as useless as Plato's absurd illusions about a 'perfect society'. *En tout les cas*, Marx was *un Boche* wasn't he? And *par dessus le marché,* he spent years reading books in the British Library in London, would you believe it? Oh no, the Russians won't be taken in by his *conneries* for very long. *Vous verrez!*

Of course the Germans are far too *raisonnable* to have taken Marx and the other chap, what's his name, Engels — another *Boche* if you please — well *they* don't take it at all seriously. Look at what Adolf Hitler, Der Führer the Germans call him, look what he's doing for Germany, all those roads — the autobahns. It's amazing what that man has accomplished in so short a time. They say he uses convicts as labourers, well it's a lot better than having them sitting in their cells *jouer de la mandoline* and wasting the taxpayers money, isn't it? Basil was there earlier this year and he says he was doing a hundred and twenty in the Bugatti and Vera joked about how young Rupert thought he could jump out and run alongside the car. You simply don't get an impression of speed on these autobahns, the surfaces are as smooth as a billiard table.

Remember how all the Germans had to carry that *torch cul* paper money of theirs in wheelbarrows just to buy a loaf of bread? It was *foutrement con*. Well, Hitler is changing all that quickly enough isn't he? That *emmerdeur* Winston Churchill keeps warning everybody that Hitler is a power-mad lunatic who wants to become ruler of the world. It's upsetting the Germans no end and King George or someone ought to keep Winston quiet and tell him to mind his own business.

Mind you, one can't help wondering how Hitler with his funny little moustache — just like Charlie Chaplin's, isn't it *tordant* — how he got into power so quickly. But of course he must have been helped by those tough Brown Shirt bully boys of his in the Nazi Party going around banging everyone on the head who opposed their precious Der Führer. But that's politics for you isn't it.

Yes admittedly Hitler has made these claims about wanting bits of Poland returned to Germany, but they belonged to *Les Boches* in the first place, didn't they, until the Allies messed around with the borders after the war, so he's being perfectly reasonable about it. And all this talk about his being power mad and wanting to conquer everything and become Ruler of the World, well frankly he's got his plate full with getting Germany properly organized so he simply hasn't got time to go gallivanting around conquering the rest of the world, it's so silly. Besides you know, the Russians would never go along with anything like that. They'd stop him dead in his tracks.

Everyone should pay more attention to that chap Chamberlain, he's very sensible and he's got the right perspective on the situation. He's not losing his nerve and wasting money on armaments and getting the stock exchange in a panic that would start another Depression. It was bad enough last time, remember, when Ronnie Goldberg threw himself out of the window of his Wall Street office on the fifteenth floor. Good tennis player he was, too. Such a waste. No, if there's going to be a war it'll probably start like the last time with some idiotic assassination in the Balkans or somewhere like that. Well anyway it's all very unlikely.

*   *   *

And so they went on talking about world affairs — that's
when they were not gossiping about the extramarital affairs
of absent friends or holding a postmortem on a recent game
of bridge. And when I asked them what a Ruler of the
World was, they patted me on the head and told me that it
was a man who told everyone in the world when it was time
to eat and when it was time to go to bed. That last remark
about going to bed made everyone laugh but I couldn't see
anything funny about that, which made them laugh even
more. Grown-ups, I had decided, were not all that *amusant*.
And now, sixty years later, I have no reason to alter my
opinion.

I have given a lot of thought to the question of why some
individuals have such extraordinary power over everyone
else around them, and I think I may have found the answer.
It is: sulking. They can indulge in massive sulks, which
then forces everyone to pander to them because most
people can't tolerate an unpleasant atmosphere for very
long. It's as simple as that.

And I have also occasionally reflected on what I would do
if I were Ruler of the World. Well, doesn't everyone?

The Teacher

Shortly before the war my father was appointed lecturer in
English at the Fuad el Awal University in Cairo. He relished
teaching grammar and idiomatic English to his Egyptian
students because he believed that it was the most beautiful
language of all and that it had been bequeathed to the world
by an erudite God who shared his appreciation of its
richness — with special regard for the splendour of its
adjectives, which it was not unfashionable to use with some
abandon in those days, and for the elegance, variety and wit
of its Grammar, Syntax, and Figures of Speech. Faced with
the choice, my father may well have hesitated for a split
second before placing his hand on the Holy Bible rather
than on Fowler's Modern English Usage before swearing
an oath. He had a devout interest in philology which, I hope
you will forgive me for pointing out, means: the science of
language. After all, it's not a word we hear every day —
we don't often hear people casually saying 'I have a devout
interest in philology'. At least, I don't think so.

I was about eleven years old when my father suddenly
announced that I should learn to be fluent in English, my
paternal native tongue. I cannot be sure of the precise
reason for that decision, but it may have been due to the
fact that if I was eventually to go to an English university,
as he hoped, my almost complete ignorance of the language
would most certainly turn out to be a severe handicap.

My father was a very methodical person. He enroled me for
a Berlitz crash course in spoken English and gave me a
brand new copy of Charles Dickens' Martin Chuzzlewit, as
well as The Concise Oxford Dictionary and his own leather
bound set of the plays of William Shakespeare. He had
evidently entertained the notion that I was to be thrown in
at the deep end on a fairly high literary note.

Some months later he handed me a magnificent illustrated
edition of The Adventures of Baron Munchausen as a
reward for having raced through the previous tomes —
well, not *all* of them, but I had enjoyed Hamlet and the
Merchant of Venice in an idiosyncratic sort of way: at first
like a cryptographer painstakingly deciphering a tantalizing
alien message. And then, when I came to recognize the
many echoes and familiar sights of latin roots shared with
the French language, the meanings of words became clear
and the fluency and rhythm with which that message was
composed entranced me. I never made it to university, and
my spoken English, I am told, is quirky, so it probably
unconsciously bears traces of that slightly unusual
introduction to the language.

My mother, on the other hand, had made it clear that she
found little merit in a language that most men spoke with
a tobacco pipe clenched between their teeth. That was, of
course, in the days when most English gentlemen spoke
without moving their lips and with a pipe clenched firmly
between their teeth. Pipes were important in those days.
They were a symbol of reliability, stability, strength of
character, moral fibre, and a calm and undemanding nature
— all the qualities of an English gentleman, at heart if not
in social status. Gigolos and pansies, it was generally
understood, were positively not pipe smokers.

I used to watch with fascination when my father scraped
the clinker out of his pipe bowl and rodded the mixture of

nicotine and saliva out of the stem with a short length of wire twisted around cotton wool. He would sometimes pat me affectionately on the head when he had completed the ritual.

Yet the whole manly business seemed to trouble my mother, because she would walk out of the room declaring that it was *'insupportable'* and she would withdraw for several hours to her boudoir with a migraine. She explained to me about forty-five years later, shortly after my father's death, and as we were agonizing over what to do with his collection of pipes, that what had set her teeth on edge was the *sounds*: the gurgling of the salivary slurry as he blew down the stem; the scraping off of the clinker, like a knife drawn across glass; and finally, the tap-tapping of the inverted bowl against the side of his pewter ashtray. She had also been extremely irritated by the imploding little 'mmupm mmupm' noise he made as he drew the first few puffs after packing the bowl to just the right density with tobacco, lighting it, and enveloping his head in a cloud of smoke. It had puzzled me at the time that such a curiously innocent activity should give so much blissful pleasure to one person when it was so maddening to a spectator. I later realized that this was only one of the many small things in life that can be insupportable to a lot of people.

My father gave me one of his most treasured pipes some years later when I was eighteen years old and I think that this may have been part of my initiation into manhood as far as he was concerned. I was on leave from the air force at the time and spending a few days with my parents. Later that day, he invited me to his study and, after we were seated, handed me his soft leather tobacco pouch which was lined with yellow oil-cloth to preserve the moisture in the shredded leaf. He addressed me in English with an air of edgy insouciance:

"Have a try at that dear boy, mixture of Erinmore and Africander — reasonably cool on the tongue"

"Thank you sir, but not right now if you'll excuse me" I replied politely " Maman has prepared her special blanqette d'agneau for our dinner and I was aiming to keep my palate fresh for the occasion"

A small muscle rippled in my father's cheek as he paused in order to compose himself before replying: "No no no, my dear boy. . . you must aim *AT*. . . it's like a target don't you see? Good heavens, you cannot aim *TO* a target! Now where was I? Ah yes. . . well now, I take it that you have. . . that you know about. . . what I mean is that now that you are a man *soit disant*. . . that you should know about men and women and. . . and having babies, of course. I daresay that you have given some thought to. . . to. . . les demoiselles, *donc j'éspère que vous comprenez ce que je veux dire?*"

I suddenly realized that the old man was at that very moment agonizing over the problem of how to go about his paternal duty of acquainting me with the details of one of the crucial facts of life — and that he was totally, preposterously unaware of the fact that he was. . . by many more years than I could remember. . . a little too late. What could I say?

"Yes, thank you sir"

It seemed an inadequate reply to me, but it presumably set his mind at rest on that score, because he had muttered: "Splendid, splendid. Well, that settles it then. Now you should have a word with Polonsky. . . he's the right chap for. . . you know. . . les demoiselles"

He slipped a tightly folded five guinea note into my uniform shirt pocket, made a disconcerting attempt at a wink and then started to wind his wristwatch — an indication that the awkward interview was at an end.

It now dawned on me that what my father had in mind was my ultimate initiation into manhood and that Polonsky was to be the entrepreneur in charge of that primal rite. I tried hard to imagine what my wife would have made of all this, but she had been abducted some weeks before by her two brothers during one of my absences on active duty, and I had not been able to trace her whereabouts. It had been the final drastic move by her wealthy and powerful Egyptian family which confirmed the fact that I was not considered a suitable or permanent match for their only daughter. There was a war on and they may, after all, have been right. It had been a secret wedding, and neither of my parents was aware of that aspect of my life since I had not wanted to cause my mother unnecessary concern. In view of her nervous condition it might have precipitated the most dramatic migraine of all time. Or perhaps the main reason had been that I was unwilling to receive any advice which did not suit me.

Polonsky, I shall explain briefly, was a young man who was obsessively devoted to my mother. His own parents had remained in Poland before the war, while he had been sent to stay with an aunt in Egypt. And now his parents had vanished, and his elderly aunt was dead, and he had found the protective comfort and companionship in my mother of which he had been cruelly deprived by the same terrible events that had tragically affected so many lives. My mother, in turn, had discovered a dutiful, compliant and continuously grateful substitute son. I too was grateful for the filial attention he gave to her, which, because of my tours of duty, I was unable to provide.

That kindly young man, who was only a little older than myself, had another side to his nature: he had a fanatical

desire to become a Hollywood film star and had no doubt
whatsoever that he would succeed in his goal as soon as the
war was over. He had albums of movie actors' and
actresses' photographs, many of them autographed to him
personally, and he kept a card index in which he entered all
the personal information he could possibly obtain about all
the stars. He felt very close to them and referred to them
quite unselfconsciously by their first names as though they
were intimate friends of his. I remember that he was fairly
confident that Lana Turner would be his leading lady in his
first starring role. Like so many dreams, this one, as far as
I know, was to remain unfulfilled. In later years it became
a habit of mine to keep an eye open for Polonsky in all the
Hollywood movies I watched. . . I would seek his pale
round baby-face and light blond hair among the extras in
battle scenes, in crowd scenes in streets, subways, circuses,
hotel lobbies, nightclubs, and even in crowded stadiums. I
would peer at the screen in Western movies. . . was he on
horseback, or a drunk at the bar or a card player in a
saloon? A snub-nosed Polish Redskin brave? . . Hollywood
movies were great at miscasting in those days. But if he
was there, somewhere, as I'm sure he must have been, I
never caught a glimpse of him.

He had another, more immediate abiding passion. He was
a regular and favoured patron of the most select *maison
close* in town, as I discovered after I had informed him that
very evening of my father's well-intentioned subscription
to what turned out to be a memorable soirée's entertainment
under Polonsky's enthusiastic tutelage.

*   *   *

Two years after the war had ended I visited my parents at
their jasmine farm near Grasse in the south of France,

where they had decided to settle down. My father and I were doing the Sunday Times crossword puzzle one warm summer evening, seated at a pinewood table beneath the persimmon tree.

The fireflies were flicking their little lights on and off all around us and the scent of the jasmine flowers in the fields was almost overpowering as I struggled with an intractable clue. My father removed his glasses — he had put away his pince-nez when he joined the Royal Air Force — and after rubbing his eyes and replacing his glasses, he gave me a smile that informed me that he had found the answer. However, courteous as always, he was not going to deprive me of the satisfaction of making my own discovery. Instead, still smiling in a way I had not seen before, he said: *'Remember, my boy, that Confucius once made the observation that a man has no way of becoming a gentleman unless he understands Destiny; he has no way of taking his stand unless he understands the rites; and above all, that he has no way of judging men unless he understands words'.*

I have always tried to understand how other men understood words — only they sometimes called them something else, like 'linguistics'. They wrote a lot of words about words and about language and it was all so incomprehensible that I wondered how they could possibly have understood what they themselves had written.

But I have always remembered that my father, who had always been a gentleman, although not always successful in judging men, had most certainly understood words. And that is what he taught me.

The Culprit

I discovered early in my childhood that parents and other grown-ups could be very obstinate in thwarting perfectly reasonable requests, usually on grounds that were wholly unreasonable. Now, a child endowed with a determination sharpened on the whetstone of survival of the fittest, or loudest, will persevere until success is achieved. The object of desire may then be acquired, or failing that, at least some prickly attention — which is appeasing when it confirms to the child that his or her existence is being acknowledged. The supreme importance of acknowledgement by others of our existence persists throughout our lives, and it may explain our passion for achievement as well as much of our sometimes peculiar behaviour. This will, of course, not apply quite so obviously to hermits, who tend to be unsociable people and who may have been smothered with love when they were very young.

Sometimes a child's persistent provocation of its parent is not simply the superficial 'cry for love' that it is often assumed to be. It is a primitive and instinctive test of efficient guardianship. In other words, if the parent can be driven to respond self-defensively to the child's vexatious behaviour, then that parent has, by the same token, demonstrated the capability of protecting the child against danger from others. You will find that most mammals do this; but it is only with humans that the parent's anger sometimes spills over into violence, thereby causing terror, or lethal damage, instead of providing the reassurance the child was innocently seeking in the first place. All children would prefer other ways to feel secure than by being driven into provoking righteous anger in an adult — especially when the habit of bedeviling others for that purpose may also persist throughout one's life. Am I digressing again? Oh, I'm *moralising*. Yes, I see. . .

Well, my mother very rarely smacked me, and when she did do so, it was purely her panic-stricken spontaneous reaction to my having injured myself. She was extremely sensitive, and would have preferred accidents not to take place, and if they did, then preferably not brought inconsiderately to her attention. I remember the occasion when, seated calmly on the terrace sipping her camomile *tisane*, she was startled by my noisy intrusion with an impressive abrasion on my forehead and a bloody nose — the climax to an adventurous escapade with the Bedouin children. She cried out: *Dieu du ciel!*, leaned forward, and slapped my face and then my backside.

Her tears of remorse that immediately followed were mingled with reproaches at my being the cause of her constant maternal anguish. Eager to spread the blame for her misfortune, she clasped her hands heavenward in a gesture of reprimand to a Maker who, she declared, was inexcusably neglectful of his duty to protect little children. It was a deeply moving performance, which was given added dramatic impetus by my own bravura sobbing.

Mahroos, having been alerted by the all too familiar sounds of distress, had fetched a bowl of soapy water and a wad of cotton-wool. Soapy water was the panacea in our household for a variety of ailments, and it was usually administered with ceremonial panache by my mother. My father once confided to me, many years later, that he had always been reluctant to complain of some minor illness because it invariably led to the remedy of warm soapy water being siphoned into him under protest in a manner that did little to enhance his dignity.

My mother attended to my injuries with great tenderness and consoling murmurs before inviting me to recover in her boudoir. I was to rest on cushions she placed on the floor, beside the chaise longue on which she was about to recline and stoically endure a migraine that promised to last appreciably longer than usual. Yes, this was the kind of incident that made her life an endless torment. . . *un supplice éternel.* . . she had sighed, before drifting into a slow-breathing restful slumber.

*   *   *

I found out, when I was sent to school, that grown-ups in positions of authority would routinely punish by causing physical pain. They did so with a solemn expression and an ill-concealed relish while explaining how much it grieved them. The teachers at the French school would rub a thumb hard across a boy's ear as a mark of disapproval while shaking their heads and pursing their lips with sadness. And when I was a little older and attending an English school, I soon discovered that administering a sound drubbing on the backside with a whippy four foot long reed cane, which made a satisfying swishing sound as it swung through its arc, made the teachers quite mournful during the process. 'Spare the rod and spoil the child' is an enduringly sentimental motto, and there will always be those who believe it to be true. Perhaps they might even enjoy being caned. I wouldn't know about that because I *certainly* never enjoyed it.

However, there was one memorable occasion when I was deliberately *not* caned for my misbehaviour.

The misdemeanour took place during the performance of the boarders' end-of-term play in which I acted the part of Chorus in a spoof Greek tragedy. Instead of chanting my narrative comments from the traditional scroll, it had been agreed with our English Literature teacher, who had written and was directing the play, that I should read from a toilet roll. While the appeal of the scatological humour was irresistible to the boys in the audience, the headmaster felt otherwise as he sat stony-faced in the front row.

When I was summoned to his study three days later, he informed me that my conduct had been so odious, especially in the presence of his lady wife and the women teachers, that he had been forced to agonize for the past three days over some suitable punishment for the worst example of foul-minded conduct he had ever come across in his teaching career. He had reluctantly come to the conclusion that awarding me the maximum penalty of ten strokes of the cane would hardly be adequate in view of the severity of my offence. Moreover, he pointed out as he straightened his shoulders, expulsion had to be ruled out now on the grounds that my father was a Commissioned Officer in His Majesty's Royal Air Force and to disgrace him by sacking his son from school at a time of war would be decidedly unpatriotic. He was left with no choice, he declared with a piercing look of distaste, than to assume that the unsavoury episode had never taken place. "I have nothing more to say. Go" he muttered as he gestured toward the door. And then he added: "You have ceased to exist as far as I am concerned"

On the following day it became clear to me that he had instructed the entire staff of the school to ignore my presence completely. What he had clearly failed to take into account in making that heavy-laden decision was that if I did not exist, neither could I be punished.

There would be no point in describing in too much detail all the escapades that followed, because it can reasonably be assumed that I then embarked on a fascinating exploratory adventure of breaking all the school rules of conduct short of vandalism, arson and outright larceny. I would periodically drop in randomly at various classrooms out of bravado or whenever I felt bored; broke bounds regularly to visit the local open-air cinema and return to the school well after midnight; lie in bed until quite late in the morning and, after a hot shower, drop in to the staff kitchen for a hearty breakfast. I also spent a good deal of my day in the cool and peaceful atmosphere of the school library, where I occasionally fell asleep on the brown leather chesterfield until awakened in time for tea by the school bell. My night-time raids of the teaching-staff drinks bar and buffet resulted in periodic attacks of severe indigestion and a life-long aversion to the mere thought of a cocktail consisting of equal measures of Scotch whisky, Bacardi rum, Gordon's gin, Cointreau and Harvey's sweet sherry, with a dash of Angostura bitters. It was an idyllic period of my life, which ended all too abruptly one day when the school closed down for the summer holidays. I was never to return.

About thirty years later at a school reunion of Old Boys and Girls held in London, that dignified headmaster, who was still in full possession of his wits, may well have failed to recognize me as, smiling at someone at the other end of the room, he walked straight past my outstretched hand.

The Cook And The Gardener

Everyone kept chickens. There were chickens everywhere. Very ordinary chickens, scratching at the hard dry earth or fluffing their feathers in the dust to rid themselves of parasites; laying eggs in the strangest places; brooding in straw nests. There were hens being chased and mounted by some scraggy rooster; others trespassing destructively in vegetable and flower gardens or roaming into houses and leaving their droppings on Indian rugs. Many would stray into the road where they were sometimes converted into a mess of mangled feathers by a passing motorcar. A few would wander on to the tramlines and not always step out of the way when a tram went by. Some roosted in the lower branches of trees while others flapped their way on to the flat roofs of garages where they would peck holes into the tarred felt. The older ones were periodically crowded into wicker coops, destined for the market place and cooking pot. Mabrooka shared her small hut with a few chickens and spoke to them with clucking sounds, which they seemed to understand because they were reasonably obedient — if one can say that about what are undoubtedly the daftest creatures on this planet.

Now my mother had a flock of Rhode Island Reds. They were kept in a caged enclosure beside the wash-house in the garden, large well-fed glossy-feathered fowl that looked marginally less idiotic than the other chickens in the neighbourhood. That was the opinion expressed by my

father, and his judgement on these matters was one to be
respected at all times. This must also have been a source
of minor satisfaction for my mother, whose opinion of
Madame Mimi Ferguson's chickens was that their intellect
did not fall far short of their owner's powers of reasoning.

Monsieur Guillaume Petit was into eggs. He collected them.
He described with passion their functional efficacy and
perfection, their fundamental aesthetic attributes and their
widespread influence on all architecture. He philosophised
about their allegorical significance in the arts, and he
emphasised their mystical and sexual symbolism as well as
their ritualistic importance in all religions and cultures
throughout the ages. He marvelled at their structural
efficiency and their radial symmetry. He theorised about
their medicinal properties and nutritional value, and he
rhapsodised over the endless ways of preparing them — not
to mention the crucial role they played in the creation of
omelettes, soufflés, sauces, mayonnaise, confectionery and
so many other divine blessings to the human palate. In
short, eggs were his inspiration. Madame Petit, sadly, was
not in the least bit interested in eggs.

One afternoon Monsieur Petit rode up on his bicycle
carrying a cardboard shoe-box. It contained a birthday
present for me: a large duck egg and a much smaller
bantam's egg, wrapped in cotton wool. They were freshly
laid and fertilised, he informed me meaningfully, adding
some now long-forgotten abstruse snippet of knowledge
about avian ovaries.

After he had gone, I took the eggs to Mahroos who slipped
them under a brooding Rhode Island Red. She clucked
maternally and waggled down comfortably to perform her
surrogate role, which, for all she knew, might eventually
produce a golden eagle and a baby alligator. No matter, a
brooding hen will sit on anything more or less egg-shaped.

But how long would my two eggs take to hatch? I visited the hen daily. I became impatient. Nature was not moving fast enough for my eager curiosity. Eventually they both emerged from their shells within hours of each other: a little duckling and a minuscule bantam chick. I had an irresistible desire to pick them up and play with them, but Mahroos held me back firmly and said: "No little master, they are yours but they are not playthings. And so you may enjoy them only with your eyes. Observe them carefully"

And so I did. At first they followed the old hen and mimicked her scratching and pecking for grains. But after a few days I noticed that they had lost interest in their foster mother, and from then on they stayed very close to each other as they wandered around the large cage in search of tidbits. As they grew a little bigger, the bantam chick would sometimes ride on the duckling's back and they would keep up a continuous quack and cheep, acknowledging and reassuring each other as they made their way among the large Reds. My father named them Napoleon and Josephine. Napoleon, of course, was the bantam.

One day, my father called Mahroos and then said to me: "I want you to watch something most interesting. Please wait here my son, and do not move". He was cradling the duckling against his chest and Mahroos held the chick gently in his cupped hands as they walked in opposite directions until they were out of sight round the two visible corners of the house.

And then there were sounds I had never heard before: the continuous panic-stricken cheeping from the chick and the anguished quacking from the duckling. Suddenly the two little creatures appeared, skidding round their corners and running toward each other in a frantic sprint. Their legs were not designed by nature for such urgency and were left behind by the forward momentum of their bodies. Stumbling and falling and rolling over and over, the little yellow balls would find their feet and rush on until they fell again and then one would lose its bearings and scramble in the opposite direction, momentarily silenced by confusion over its companion's disappearance from view until the other's cries made it circle back in the right direction. Their skinny necks were craned forward, and their tiny flightless wings were stretched out and flapping, instinctively attempting to stabilize and outpace a careening centre of gravity and take to the air.

They finally collided in a mad dance in which they banged their heads together again and again in a futile attempt to intertwine their short little necks, with their cheeping and quacking mingling in a dissonant hymn of pure rapture. They went on bumping continuously into each other as though they were attempting to meld their bodies into one inseparable living being. Finally, exhausted, they folded their legs and cuddled close together panting breathlessly with their beaks wide open.

Mahroos and my father had run alongside the chick and the duckling, and had watched the extraordinary reunion. My father turned to me and asked: "Would you ever want to witness this again?"

With my lips tightly closed, I shook my head in dismay. Mahroos turned to his master with a smile and said in Arabic: "Ya'ffendi, it is as we both expected of the boy, is it not?"

*   *   *

My bantam cockerel with iridescent plumage was allowed to range freely in the orchard. The tiny rooster strutted

possessively around his entourage of four midget hens all
day, with his head held high, always keeping a watchful eye
on them, a cocked eye if you prefer, and scolding with an
authoritative squawk any who wandered away from the
group in their mindless scratching and pecking for seeds
and insects. He may have known that the feral cats and the
wild mongooses were very partial to the flesh of chickens,
or at least, his instinct for survival must have given him
some such warning and he bravely drove away any cat or
other stalker that approached his family. He and his wives
always roosted on the same branch in one of the lemon
trees, and he invariably placed himself closest to the main
trunk in order to protect the hens from attack by any
tree-climbing predator.

He fathered a countless number of offspring and lived to a
ripe old age, as far as a bantam cock's natural longevity
goes. He would always begin crowing some time before
dawn, which would start other cocks crowing throughout
the neighbourhood in a chain reaction that spread over a
radius of several miles.

Toward the end, his voice had lost much of the penetrating
high-pitched timbre that would startle dozing sparrows out
of the trees, and he finally gave up the ghost in mid-crow
one late morning. Napoleon was not consigned to the
cooking pot but carefully buried, beside his closest friend
Josephine, who had died the year before, at the foot of a
mimosa tree in full bloom. And throughout my life, mimosa
blossoms would remind me of two small creatures and the
powerful and mysterious bond that had linked them so
closely together while they were both alive.

*   *   *

Let us move on to a good many years later. I was forty-five years old, divorced and alone in a motel room's tiny kitchenette and about to do nothing less than prepare and eat, in the most civilized way, a salad sandwich. No, not a crude jumbo sandwich into which I would have to bury my face to manage a bite, but an elegant and subtly stratified invention in which the flavours would create a kind of synergy for the taste buds. . . where the total effect would reach an amalgamated culinary pinnacle rising high above the sum of its individual ingredients. If you see what I mean.

And I felt happy. Wait. What is happiness? Is it simply a transitory state that, by its very nature defies analysis, like some sub-atomic particle that vanishes if you try to pin it down? It is certainly a fleeting emotion because if it were permanent it wouldn't be true happiness but a kind of euphoria in which the senses are not heightened but dull — like a permanently smiling face. On the other hand I did not feel exactly cheerful. No, not the way we all felt cheerful on those occasional Sunday afternoons in our home in California when I had a family of my own.

We would sit on the terrace and have cucumber and smoked salmon sandwiches and scones for tea, and my father, who was staying with us, had on one occasion declared with great dignity, as though at a prize-giving ceremony: *'You have made a perfect pot of tea, Contessa, and furthermore, your sandwiches are most civilized and your scones are the food of angels.'* That praise was addressed to our cook Inconsolata, who responded to his little speech with a delighted cry of: *'Aiee, Madonna Santa, Commendatore. . . lei mi dice una cosa cattivella in Inglese!'* as she swung her generous hips with astonishing daintiness in step with a brilliantly sustained obbligato of giggles all the way to the kitchen, on one single intake of breath, and into the back garden where she regaled Katsuo, our inscrutable Japanese gardener, with an appreciation in Italian of my father's waggish humour. Katsuo would, in such circumstances, remain inscrutable since he understood not one word of that alien language.

Ah, how well I remember Inconsolata's gnocchi: now they were a perfect example of her passionate observance of a traditional recipe. She may have allowed herself the occasional minor frivolous deviation from the well established range of ingredients that her mother had taught her to incorporate in some classic sauce, true enough, but if it had been decreed that gnocchi had to be made *'con pomodoro, non con semolina per l'amor di Dio'*. . . then so be it. Besides, gnocchi lovingly and skilfully made with just the right kind of waxy potatoes, boiled and mashed to a fine glutinous paste, then rolled lightly in flour, curled into small shells with a fork and dropped into a pan of simmering salted water from a precise height at just the right velocity. . . she had declared that this is a form of pasta that could only have been devised by a Roman goddess for some wholly divine purpose. Gnocchi made from semolina. . . well, they simply couldn't be called gnocchi, and that was that.

Oh, and her pistachio ice-cream. Yes, she would have considered it near-blasphemy, an offence against the very purity of Nature as created by Our Most Holy Heavenly Father, to have added spinach dye, let alone a single drop of some chemical dye, to her creation in order to achieve a gaudy hue which would overwhelm the delicate tone of the real thing. . . *chemical food dyes? Dio mio! Was there no limit to Man's perfidiousness?*

Oh yes, and her pine resin ice cream: she had once confided in me that the secret method for making that most exotic of all gelati had been disclosed to her by a Turkish

confectioner on his deathbed. The accompanying wink and
smirk had suggested a somewhat more intimate didactic
encounter — ah, but Inconsolata was one of life's great
hinters, beyond which secrecy was unassailably preserved.
Like her gnocchi, the pine resin ice-cream she created
formed adhesive strands that stuck tantalisingly to one's
lips. It would dissolve very slowly in the mouth and release
its essences at its own pace while powerfully sustaining
one's pleasure in those aromas until a point of ecstasy of
the palate was eventually reached which, in the opinion of
the aficionados who were privileged to savour it, was
infinitely superior to another carnal delight.

Inconsolata had a coterie of admirers among the local men,
each of whom would sometimes linger at the back door
after making a delivery, in the hope of receiving a taste of
one of her sweet concoctions. She claimed that a blind
person could guess their occupations by the faint aroma that
surrounded them: Big Billy Levitt was motor oil; Sandy
Parris fresh bread; Joe Harper was meat. Mr Morris
Samuelson was definitely fish she would declare, wrinkling
her expressive nose to emphasise the point.

Those steadfast admirers of hers were well past middle age,
with wives and adolescent children, but the innocent sport
of flirting with Inconsolata never lost its appeal. It had
become a ritual: each, when he thought no-one was looking,
would playfully prod her ample waist or pinch her posterior
as if by accident and give a humorously suggestive wink.
She would unfailingly reward him with a surreptitious
smack on the wrist and the heavenward entreaty: *'Ah, que
cattivo, ma cosa posso fare io con questo poltrone?'*. This
was accompanied by a coquettish pout that held a promise
of unspecified potential delights at the appropriate time,
delights which, needless to say, never materialized. Nor

were they ever likely to do so because that would assuredly have spoiled the innocent game for ever.

That fraternal informal order of the knights of Inconsolata would meet regularly for a beer at the local tavern. It had been the custom, always, for each in turn, to taunt the others with the merest hint that he had, at last, been chosen as her clandestine consort. This was greeted with sceptical applause but not the slightest trace of ribaldry. . . evidence of their respect for her as a very special lady, and of their unshakable and well-founded belief in her virginal purity.

Katsuo Mokubei, whose great-grand-uncle had been a famous ceramist in Kyoto, always smelt delicately of the carnation eau de toilette with which he rubbed down his whole body after soaking himself in a cedarwood tub of near-boiling water for exactly fifteen minutes at the first crack of dawn every morning. He was occasionally heard to growl from the shrubbery if he decided that one of the fellows was showing signs of becoming importunate in his attentions to the cook.

Inconsolata would occasionally interrupt a task in the kitchen to stroll out into the garden, but it was only to make sure that Katsuo — whose frail appearance belied his wiry strength — had not come to some harm, especially when he was teetering at the top of a ladder pruning a fruit tree. *'That old fool will kill himself one of these days'* she would exclaim as she peered anxiously out of the kitchen window.

She would frequently obtain choice portions of fresh raw tuna, bass, squid, or other delicacy from Mr Samuelson for Katsuo to cut expertly against the grain into *sashimi* slices which he would dip into a saucer of soy sauce spiced with *wasabi* green horseradish and then eat daintily with his lacquered chopsticks. She would occasional glance at him out of the corner of her eye and shake her head with affectionate incredulity and mock disgust at his making such a ceremonial feast out of those primitive ingredients. Raw fish! Madonna mia, her sainted mother would no doubt turn in her grave to observe such a barbaric performance, may God rest her soul.

Katsuo would, at noon precisely every day, silently deliver a peach or some other fruit ripened to perfection, freshly picked and carefully wrapped in a large leaf to preserve the freshness. He would leave it on the window-sill over the sink — thereby making it clear that it was to be enjoyed by the cook and by no one else. The daily supply of fruit, herbs and clean vegetables for the household was brought in by him early every morning, lovingly laid out in a wicker basket like a votive offering at a harvest festival. It was the gardener's personal tribute to the loving care with which, in his estimation, the cook would transform the produce he had nursed from the soil into works of art which, however transitory their existence, were nonetheless a medium for her self-expression as well as her veneration of those exquisite gifts of nature. That was the way he saw it and the way he must have felt about it.

It became clear to me that the bond of friendship between the gardener and the cook had — in spite of being formal in an almost quaintly old-fashioned way — a great deal more fibre in it than many of the more outwardly intimate relationships of some of the married couples I knew.

Although they were, the two of them, totally different in every way, there had evolved a binding kinship of spirit that could not be put into words without it being reduced to anecdotal absurdity. Yet there it was, a curious attachment and dependency, contributing its share of light into each of their days and thereby making the darker moments of remembered sadness from the past that much easier to endure.

And that silent bond between them, that powerful dependency which never needed to be confirmed by any spoken word, ended suddenly and unexpectedly one chilly overcast day when, for no good reason, Katsuo rushed out of his potting shed in terror to find the cook lying on the kitchen floor gasping for breath, one side of her face frozen in an anguished grimace as he cradled her head in his lap and cried out for help.

Inconsolata's funeral service was attended by all the family, and by Katsuo, fragrant with essence of carnation, looking small and out of context yet resplendent in sombre ceremonial garb decorated with his family *Mon* embroidered in silk and with his sword in its black lacquered sheath tucked in his broad silk waistband. Mr Samuelson and his cadaverous mother were at the service, smelling faintly of fish, mothballs, and oil of cloves. . . a remarkable combination in every sense. The other mourners, Inconsolata's band of admiring courtiers, were present, smartly dressed in identical double-breasted black suits which made them look, in a curiously appropriate fashion, like Capos from the same Sicilian Mafia 'Family'.

Katsuo was the most dramatically affected at Inconsolata's funeral. He had, at one stage of the church service, banged his forehead repeatedly on the backrest of the pew in front of him and uttered hoarse cries of anguish. Big Billy, Joe Harper and I had to escort him out of the church because the priest had lost the thread of his funeral oration and was frowning silently in our direction. Once outside, Katsuo had drawn his sword and had to be further restrained in his attempt to sever, in a spontaneous act of immolation, the neatly rolled-up scroll of hair on the crown of his head. We did not altogether appreciate his action, since it certainly appeared as though he was about to attempt the bizarre feat of beheading himself from the rear. In the ensuing struggle to disarm him, Big Billy suffered a cut on his thumb that required five stitches but which also placed him in the enviable position for the rest of his life of boasting almost truthfully that he had been wounded by a Japanese Samurai wielding his sword in a rage. . . and that he had miraculously survived the encounter. Such was the stuff of local legends.

After her sudden death they never met again at the tavern. Mr Samuelson's aged mother fell off her bicycle a month later and died from pneumonia, followed by Mr Samuelson himself from a fatal stroke a few weeks after that. The black funeral suits were by then beginning to look a trifle crumpled.

Katsuo continued to take his ritual scalding bath every morning, and had taken up the habit of knocking back, throughout the day, dainty sake-cupfuls of Johnny Walker Black Label Whisky, mulled to just above body temperature on the potting shed wood stove. This resulted in the addition of a swaying sideways roll to his stooped lolling trot, which, together with the forward clutching motion of his hands, created the impression that he was trying to catch up with his own centre of gravity weaving out of reach a few paces ahead of him. The effect was further enhanced by the baggy Japanese pants that he always wore during the day. It was a memorable performance of unique and unconscious originality that would have ranked high at the top of the bill among the immortals of comedy in the days of vaudeville. Moreover he had never been observed to fall flat on his face. . . a masterly feat of acrobatic control. He lived on for a few more years after the loss of Inconsolata, until his death while on the operating table for the removal of a painful impacted wisdom tooth which, he had been warned, may in all likelihood become infected and cause him even greater chronic discomfort.

That old man had, for almost forty years, mourned in solitude over a young wife killed in a bombing raid during the war. Had he savoured his brief term of happiness with her so deeply that it sustained him for the rest of his life? Perhaps. Or had the bitter aloe of his loss shrivelled his heart with its astringency? No, not Katsuo, that gentlest of men. He somehow managed to transmute that innate love into the formalized and disciplined ritual of his own formula for living.

Inconsolata had, in her own unique way, given him the kind of respect that provided him with the knowledge that he was important as a human being and, even more, that he was needed by others. He had never been with another woman after the loss of his bride and he kept a large framed photograph of her in his quarters above the garage. I can remember one room so clearly: the *tatami* room in which Katsuo performed the tea ceremony; the *chadana* in which were stored those exquisite cups made by his great-grand-uncle, the tea-making utensils, and the bamboo tea whisk, its end split into such fine slivers that it looked like my father's shaving brush; the *hibachi*, with its charcoal embers. And in the corner, the *tokonoma* alcove with the framed *sumi-e* ink painting of a *tanuki*, the legendary badger priest, that I had painted as a gift to him. Yes, Katsuo had patiently taught me Japanese calligraphy: how to choose the right brush, how to load it expertly with ink, and finally how to hold my breath and apply brush to rice paper with carefully modulated strokes. . . the brush as much a messenger of my inner self as it was an extension of my hand.

I remember something else: there was always one fresh flower and a leafy sprig in a small bowl in front of that photograph of the modestly smiling young girl with the appearance of a little ivory figurine in her ceremonial wedding dress. . . the daily flower eternally refreshing and bringing to life her faded sepia image.

Another framed photograph hung on the wall in a small bamboo alcove in Katsuo's room. It was of a plump young woman wearing a cook's apron, with a nose a little too large for her smiling face, and of a solemn-looking middle-aged Japanese man by her side. They are both standing stiffly at attention — the way some people do when they are about to have their picture taken with a camera. One would perhaps notice, if one were to examine the photograph very carefully, that the cook's little finger is sticking out and touching the sleeve of the man's kimono.

The Peach Eater

I was rarely given sweets as a child because, I was told, they were bad for my teeth; but an exception was sometimes made on a rather special occasion. Nadia, the young Syrian cook who had recently joined the household, would melt a kilo of white sugar crystals in a shallow pan on the kitchen hob and add the juice from several lemons. When the candy had cooled down sufficiently, Nadia would cut off a small nugget for me to chew. She would then wet her hands and knead the large lump into several smaller lumps after which it all disappeared to her mistress's private bathroom where it would never be seen again. At least, that had been the case until the day, shortly after my seventh birthday, when I sneaked into that forbidden place in my quest to solve the mystery, and discovered a slab of that candy which was out of reach on a glass shelf above the chromed towel-rack.

I climbed onto the bathroom stool and grabbed the candy and snapped a bit off with my teeth and mnyum mnyum how wonderful it tasted. Then I ran out to my hiding place in the variegated ficus bushes in the garden in order to gorge myself in private on the tangy sweetness of the rest of that large chunk of stolen treasure. But my ecstasy was short-lived after that first bite and a few days later I was unable to resist confiding my wicked secret to Nadia. . . if only to find out how you could end up with a ball of short hairs in your mouth after sucking delicious home-made lemon-flavoured candy.

And now, all these years later, I remember my mother and Nadia chuckling for days over my bewildering encounter with their traditional and painfully effective depilatory device. I have since wondered how much of an analytical case history the worthy Doctor Sigmund Freud would have made of that episode if he had been told about it. He would no doubt have found a clear connection between certain predilections and aversions which in later years may have affected my life in some small way or other.

*   *   *

Mahroos would sometimes beckon me toward one of the fruit trees in the small orchard and hold me up so that I could reach a fruit that was ripe for picking. I had been warned many times not to pick and eat certain fruits or berries from the garden because they were very bad for me and I would probably die if I put them in my mouth. That's what they kept telling me, but I found that explanation unconvincing, and saw it as a challenge to my spirit of adventure. . . and still one more forbidden thing that the adults were permitted to do with impunity. It was — like so many things they did — most unreasonable.

Now, in one of the flower borders in our garden there was a large capsicum shrub that bore a multitude of small pods all the year round. These pods festooned the shrub in a variety of shades of yellow, orange, red, and green, like small coloured marbles.

One day they finally became irresistible and I boldly plucked a shiny crimson one, popped it into my mouth and bit into its crisp flesh. A fire was suddenly lit on my tongue,

dozens of hot needles pierced the tender flesh of the inside
of my cheeks, and my lips felt as though they were being
stung by a million small ants. The sap from the crushed
chili pod mingled with my saliva and ran searingly down
my throat like molten lead. It took my breath away for the
few seconds that I was in shock and then I let out a scream
of agony and fear that brought my mother, Tantine Frida,
Nadia and Mahroos running panic-stricken to my side.

They washed my mouth out with soapy water and rinsed it
with sugared water and then they gave me a banana to eat
with some fresh white bread. It was one of the rare
occasions when I was not punished for my disobedience. I
never helped myself to anything in the garden again without
permission from Mahroos.

*   *   *

'You must savour it now, right away, for its essence is
fugitive' — I remembered those words as I stood alone in
the motel kitchenette in California and opened a can of
peaches to eat on the beach. Yes, it had been on a cloudless
day such as this when I walked round the high walled fruit
garden after lunch, while my father was taking a nap on the
terrace.

I found myself standing before the familiar old peach tree,
a perfectly symmetrical espalier, its branches tied to
horizontal bamboo staves with raffia ribbons, each with a
neat butterfly knot. As I was admiring Katsuo's
unmistakably fastidious expertise, and eyeing longingly the
velvety ripening peaches which decorated the outstretched
boughs, I spied the old gardener trotting erratically toward
me from a distance, with his arms dangling loosely by his
sides. He came to a halt a few feet away and bowed low

from the hip while I, bowing respectfully with my head, addressed him thus, as usual:

"Greetings Katsuo-san. You seem to be growing ageless, like my favourite Temple Pine Bonsai by the pond, the one you gave to me the day we first met. You are in good health today?"

"Greetings Edodu-san" — that is the only way he could pronounce my name — "and you are growing tall like a giant cedar tree. Tell me, is it cold up there. . . does it snow on your head? Ho ho! I am well, except for the bad-tempered little Oni demon who hammers at my tooth to cause me much pain. But I quieten him with the Jonni Wokka Whisky which Pappa-san gave me, and then the Oni leaves me in peace for a while"

"It is good. But you must see the doctor soon, because the Jonni Wokka alone will not get rid of the Oni. Ah, I see that our friend the peach tree welcomes me with it's open arms. . ."

"It does so because I have trained it to rejoice in disciplined growth and to show its fruit proudly to its partner, the sun, and to the one who appreciates its beauty"

"I see, and thus it rewards you with its fruit which carry the riches it draws from the sun and the earth. I appreciate its beauty too, so may I share in one of those juicy rewards?"

"No, Edodu-san, only I can receive that reward. . ." the old man replied pleasantly as though citing some divine authority to whom only he was answerable. But after a short pause, during which he had studied my face with almost closed eyes while remaining expressionless, he then nodded and smiled, adding: ". . . Hai, but you may partake of my pleasure in that reward. . . for then the pleasure is trebled: it is given, it is received, and its flavour is mutually shared with the earth"

"With the earth? Indeed, that must be very wise and true. . ."

"Ho, you may mock me Edodu-san, for you could have taken the fruit without my consent because it is your tree and you are my master. But it is only your tongue that would have profited, and not too well. For only I know which peach is truly ready, and then it shall be your spirit and as well as my labour which will be sweetened by the juice of that fruit. . . here, I have chosen this one for you. You will observe that it is not the largest, but it is at the tip of the bough and contains as much aromatic nectar as its larger sisters. It has been eager to ripen earlier and to attract the carriers of its seed sooner so that it may stand a better chance of bearing a new tree and, in turn, of becoming an ancestor. Look now, how it yields to a gentle pull from my hand. . . it is ready, and you must savour it now, right away, for its essence is fugitive"

"I do not mock you Katsuo-san, for you are my master in all things that grow from the soil, but you are also a sentimental old poet. . . is it not so?"

"Here, eat it now, young man, or you will also have a taste of this sentimental old gardener's terrifying fury!"

And this little old man in his baggy pants, whose head barely reached my shoulder, stood boldly with his right leg planted firmly forward and with both hands gripping an imaginary sword handle, while I noisily sucked the warm aromatic sap and succulent firm flesh of the small round rapidly disappearing supreme glorification of that warrior-gardener's art. And when I had finished and licked my fingers and was rolling the peach stone in my mouth in order to leach out the nutty zest of the kernel it contained,

Katsuo held out his hand to receive the hard wet object. We both burst out laughing at the whole private ceremony, and then Katsuo suddenly and wordlessly bowed and started to trot toward his potting shed, no doubt eager to plant the little seed stone in a pot as the first step on its long journey to ancestorhood. Moreover, it should be known that a Samurai does not in any circumstances display his tears to a worthy young man, nor, must it be noted, does a sentimental old poet prolong a precious moment beyond its allotted time, for, as the freshly picked peach rapidly loses its essence — so might that moment lose its dignity.

The Beachcomber

When I was a small boy my father would sometimes take me for a walk along the beach very early in the morning before breakfast. Occasionally he would relate a brief anecdote about a member of his family, and at other times he would appear to be thinking out loud about things I would sometimes find hard to understand. Mostly we would walk along the shore, my hand in his, silently savouring these moments of special companionship.

He could not have said much about his own father, who had been a wealthy cotton broker and who had died many years before I was born, because, in fact, he knew very little about him. My father had been sent to boarding school in England when he was a child and had never seen my grandfather again.

All he seemed to know about his parents was that his father Henry Thorne Garnett had married a first cousin, Isabella Murray Peel — a grand-niece of Sir Robert Peel — and that they often played backgammon. He had been told by an elder brother that my grandfather, who was normally mild in temperament and never raised his voice, had thrown the backgammon board out of the window in a fury after losing a game with my grandmother late one night and had gone for a walk in the garden to cool off. He caught bronchial pneumonia and died suddenly five days later. It was then discovered that he had recently been bankrupted by the

Great Depression. All that my father inherited was the backgammon board.

He also told me about his sister Lucy who used to go tiger hunting in India and how two of his elder brothers had travelled out there many years before to rescue her from her husband, a British Army officer, who would get violently drunk and give my poor Aunt Lucy a thrashing for no better reason than that the servants would run away when he got into that state, and she just happened to be there. Aunt Lucy was a very old lady by the time I met her, but she was also very tall, and I had wondered why she hadn't given her husband a thrashing now and then in return. She lived five tram stops away from us and kept pouter pigeons in a cage in her garden and she would take me to watch them strutting around and occasionally falling over backwards because they stuck out their chests so proudly that they lost their balance. If it was their pride they were so worried about, then toppling over and making such a big fuss by flapping their wings so ridiculously didn't seem to me to be such a good idea. It was not long before I discovered that some human beings, in a way, do much the same kind of thing.

My father told me a little about Uncle Willy's misfortunes — mainly as a result of the poor man's fondness for drink. This was his brother Willy who, the old man shyly revealed to me many years later, had been 'inordinately fond of his Indian coachman-valet, a rather pretty youth who wore somewhat flamboyant livery'.

I remember my ebullient uncle shortly after one of his disastrous forays in the world of business, staying with us for a short while until that night when he awakened our household by shooting at an imaginary mouse in the dining room where he had gone in search of a drink. I was the first to arrive on the scene and there was Uncle Willy, with his bloated pink face and bloodshot eyes, swaying and aiming his revolver unsteadily at another begonia blossom on the floral patterned wallpaper from which he suspected the little rodent might reappear. A wisp of smoke came out of the barrel of the revolver as he waved me impatiently away with the weapon.

Within moments, my parents, followed by Tantine Frida, Mahroos and Nadia the cook, rushed into the room. It was a memorable tableau: Willy standing there in his paisley dressing gown, looking sheepish; my father prodding the bullet hole in the wallpaper with a look of mild disapproval; Frida, Mahroos and Nadia standing wide-eyed and speechless; and my Mother pointing accusingly at the unfortunate fellow, with the words coming out of her mouth in a neat balloon: *"Mais vous êtes complètement fou!"*. It is French for: *'But you are completely mad'*, and a wealth of meaning somehow gets lost in the translation. Of course, Uncle Willy had to go.

And then there was Uncle Percy, who had opened a highly profitable gambling casino, in partnership with a Syrian businessman, and managed to bankrupt himself by playing unwisely — and unluckily — at his own roulette tables. His partner had finally presented him with a bundle of IOU's that substantially exceeded the value of Uncle Percy's stake in the venture. Poor Percy was, everyone concluded, a genius of such monumental ineptitude that, had he invented the wheel, he would surely have succeeded in falling under it and being crushed to death.

And then, after several more failures, Percy lost his taste as well as his ability to indulge in business ventures of any kind, let alone those that were to turn him into a millionaire. And he was finally able to pursue his passion for fishing. He would wade up to his hips in the sea off the rocks every morning and remain partially submerged in salty water until sunset, standing more and less immobile unless he was baiting his hook or taking a swig from his bottle of lemonade. At the end of the day, the skin on the lower half of his body would be white and crinkled like bleached orange peel and his legs so stiffened by cramp that he was unable to walk. He would have to spend some time rubbing them vigorously to restore the circulation and some of the skin would come off like the stuff you get when you use a rubber eraser on paper.

I remember all this because I went fishing with him a few times. After a while I would get terribly bored and splash about until Uncle Percy would tell me to stop because it frightened away the fish. That didn't make much sense to me because he hurled his fishing line far out to sea using a gigantic bamboo rod. He seldom caught anything very much larger than the fish with which he baited his hook. On one occasion, standing on the rocks, I dropped the end of my fishing line into the water just below me. Almost immediately I felt a powerful tug on the line and, with some difficulty, drew in a very large rainbow coloured fish. Uncle Percy, hearing the commotion, waded over and, with a solemn expression, picked up the flapping creature and said: "Well I'll be damned!" He then turned to me and added in French: "How did you do it, mon vieux? Tell me, how did you manage it? It's altogether fantastic. You are a genius" — treasured words indeed, for I have never since received a more touching compliment

*   *   *

Once, as my father and I were strolling on the deserted beach at daybreak, he turned to me and said: "Yesterday morning we saw the sun rise. Well my little one, let me ask you something. . . would you describe what we saw as beautiful?"

"Yes Papa"

"Do you know what beautiful means?"

"The opposite of ugly?"

"Yes and no. . . ah wait, here it comes. . ."

Once again the sun was about to appear above the curvature of the planet, but not in quite the same way as I had been shown in class with a model of the planets orbiting around a white opal glass sun that had a torchlight bulb and battery in its interior, which gave it an unimpressive pallid glow. The gaudily-painted wood planets, which were hopelessly out of scale with the sun and with one another, could be moved by hand along the rims of plywood hoops attached to the base with metal wire spokes.

The geography teacher, who, I imagine, originally set out to improve the minds of the young, had developed a deep-rooted dislike for his chosen subject, especially whenever it involved the use of anything tangible such as three-dimensional topographical models, or figures of nomadic Arabs on camels, or of Eskimos spearing seals. He disliked in particular anything with moving parts since he considered that objects which could move at greater speed than glaciers were out of harmony with the essential spirit of geography. He tolerated rivers and waterfalls, but avalanches, and volcanic eruptions were, strictly speaking, well outside his academic domain. The fragile planetary system was broken shortly after the sun's battery ran out and it was given to the school carpenter to repair. It was never seen again, but the point had been made: the sun did not rotate around the earth and the earth was definitely not shaped like a flying saucer. It was this knowledge, together with other snippets of information, which enabled me, I

believed, to piece together a not wholly inaccurate idea of
the workings of the universe.

The glowing edge of the sun now rose and blinded us
momentarily with its fierce rays as my father, shielding his
eyes, said: "There it goes again my son, there it goes again.
No no, don't look straight at it! Now, let me tell you about
what is beautiful and also about what is not beautiful, not
because it's ugly but because we should use other words to
describe it. The sunrise we have just seen was not beautiful,
it was fascinating, amazing, spectacular. . . lots of big
words like that. . . but everything about it can be explained
in terms of physics, of natural laws. We know exactly why
all the colours are the way they are and how they change,
just as we know that the song of the thrush, which may be
as complex as one of Bach's most elaborate compositions,
is no more than the automatic repetition of a sound signal
that the bird cannot avoid making. And we also know that
the colours on a butterfly's wings are not conscious designs
and solid pigments, like an artist would use, but white light
broken up into all the colours of the rainbow — it's called
refracted light. And the patterns on their wings are signals
to other butterflies, who see them with quite different eyes
from ours. We may think it's all beautiful, but that's only
because we make it so with our own eyes and our ears and
our brains. So, you see my son, it is only our participation,
what we put into things as human beings, and not nature
itself that can make things beautiful. . . in the same way as
we can make things ugly just by thinking they are ugly.
Nature may work wonders, but only human beings can
create mysterious things. . . things like works of art and
music and gods. . . all those things which cannot always be
explained in words because the words themselves may
often be mysterious. . . do you see?"

"Yes Papa" I replied, eager for his approval "I think I do. Things are only beautiful if we are there to see them?"

He leaned down, looked at me through his pince-nez with great seriousness and said: "You could say that. Come to think of it son, you may have said it all"

We walked over to the old timber pier and spotted the small black crabs nibbling at the tender algae growing on the stanchions, a few inches above and below the tide line. We watched for some time as the sea-swell alternately immersed the crabs in brine and then left them exposed to the air, and I was intrigued by their apparent indifference to the rhythmic changes of medium to which they were subjected. And I threw a few small pebbles at them — not to injure them in any way, but in order to encourage them to move up and down with the swell. That would have been more logical behaviour for the crabs as far as I was concerned. But it was only a game, one in which I hoped they would participate in the proper spirit of fun and of common sense. My father placed a restraining hand gently on my wrist and said: "Listen carefully my son, have you thought about how much human beings enjoy swimming under water and also flying in the air? Well, you must realize that these are things that we choose to do voluntarily for all kinds of reasons — and the main reason is for the sheer pleasure they give us, do you understand my son?"

"Yes Papa" I replied, "will you teach me how to swim under water and to fly one day?"

"Yes, one day perhaps. . . but these little crabs over there, that's the only place they can get their food. . . and they have to adapt to the forces of nature to do so. You see, for them it's not a game, it's a matter of survival. . . of life and death. . . and we must do all we can to protect them. Now with us humans. . . especially when we are grown up. . . we sometimes get things mixed up in our minds and we cannot tell the difference between playing real games and games of life and death. Sometimes we call these games sport and sometimes we call them war and, strangest of all, we sometimes call them religion. It's quite difficult to understand, is it not young man?"

No, it had not been too hard to understand, and what's more, I had been shamed by my father's kindly reproach. I had not intended to hurt the crabs, but I was shocked by the realisation that I might have accidentally struck one of the small creatures with a pebble and killed it. A game? Life and death? Yes I understood that, and I was also greatly relieved that my aim had been so poor. I wondered earlier why my father had not joined me in the innocent sport with the pebbles, but after he had spoken so patiently, and because he was old and wise and always turned out to be right, I realized that this extraordinary man, to whom I owed my existence, must also in a mysterious way, have been given the authority to protect the lives of those crabs — and possible that of many other living creatures. I felt safe in his company.

But. . . religion? What had religion got to do with games. . . or killing? Like many other little boys, I was to grow up and discover the answer to that question in the fullness of time. And in the fullness of time a few of my friends would lose their lives in the discovery.

*   *   *

On another occasion, walking beside my father, he spoke so gently that it was not an intrusion into the privilege of silence we had shared since we stepped onto the beach in the early morning twilight. His words seemed like an extension of that quietude that held us together as firmly and comfortingly as the large hand that folded over my own in a warm and guiding grip. The waves lapping a few feet away and my father's shoes on the wet-hardened sand were the only sounds I could hear.

He then whispered mysteriously: "The sea has many perfumes, you know. Look, it is cool and calm now and smells of iodine, do you recognize the smell? And it's like fresh fish baked with herbs, too. That's the kelp, there, look, there's a patch of it floating on the surface, can you see it? You can smell it, my son, can't you? Yes. And in a few hours, when the sun has warmed the sea, it will be different. . . then you can close your eyes and think hard, think really hard, and you'll be able to smell the fish and all the other living things in the sea. . . a crisp smell, like fresh fruit. . . *fruits de mer*. . . you understand, son?"

"Yes Papa. What happens when they die?"

"Well, they get eaten up by all the tiny creatures before they start to rot and make a bad smell, like they do sometimes in the fish market. But you'd never get that smell from the sea. . . now would you?"

"No Papa"

"Now when the sea gets stormy, you get a different perfume. . . it is pungent, it tingles in your nose. . . that's because the sea makes ozone, which is a different kind of oxygen. . . are you with me son?"

"Yes Papa"

"And it makes you feel good, refreshed, raring to go. It puts energy into you. Yes, and mist at sea has its own special smell too. Why, if you were blindfolded you would still be able to tell if you were in a sea mist or a land mist. . . land mist smells of damp earth and mildewed leaves, as well as some pretty unpleasant things at times. . . but sea mist is like an ocean ghost enveloping the whole world around you. . . and you can barely smell its clean breath as it rests lightly on the sea and helps to calm its surface. Yes, and as you get older, you will discover that the sea has other aromas. . . hard to understand and very different. . . and like the very best of perfumes that some women use to entice men into their deceptive shallows, the sea contains some foul and dreaded elements to spice its sweetest essences. . . then it draws men out in boats to be swallowed up and lost for ever in its savage gales. Perhaps you didn't understand all of that, did you son?"

"No Papa, but it made me think, it really did"

"Good. You must be careful with the sea but never afraid"

"I'm not afraid when I'm with you"

My father replied: "That is how it should be, and you are a good little boy, indeed you are. Well now. . . listen carefully, you can also get the overwhelming flavour of belonging, the taste of a special kind of happiness from the sea. . . a legacy from that watery green world from which we first emerged and to which we could never return after we lost our gills. We came from the sea my son, that's where we humans came into being right at the start of life itself, and we shall always carry deep within us the hidden thirst for our birthplace under the sea. . . to be a part of it and to fly weightlessly in it. And the tears we shed to wash away our hurts are salty like the ocean, they have the perfume of sorrow and of wistful longing"

My father told me many other things during our walks along the beach. They lie buried in my unconscious, emerging at times unexpectedly, and they are then very real and delightful for me.

* * *

'I'm not afraid when I'm with you'. I remembered my
words forty-two years later, standing alone on that very
same beach just before day-break, before the sun had risen
to burn away the night mist. In the distance, infra-red
feathers of cloud were edged with purple where they
touched the grey-blue sky; the yellow horizon line was
topped by a pale green halo that blended into a lambent blue
layer of sky above. The sea, becalmed, unevenly reflected
the radiant spectrum of those backdrop colours, like a
rippled mirror without a palette of its own. It was, I could
not help thinking, all so subtly yet dramatically composed
as to seem contrived by a stage designer with an
irrepressible sentimental affection for J.M.Turner's large
seascapes. That scene lasted only another few seconds
before it was transformed by the top of the sun's glowing
corona suddenly appearing above the horizon. Quite rapidly
it became blindingly bright as though a megawatt spotlight
had been turned on me. I quickly turned my gaze away to
my right toward a hump of rocks densely matted with
mussels clustered like bunches of dull cutlery below the
tide line.

The rocks were about a hundred feet away from me,
marking the end of the sandy beach, and past the rocks I
could see the glazed terrace of that same restaurant. . . the
one where, as a young boy, I had lunched with my father.

I remembered the warm crusty bread; the mixed salad with
Italian dressing; the large prawns sautéd in garlic butter and
fresh chopped parsley; the grilled sea bass sprinkled with
squeezed green lime juice; the french fried potatoes; the
glass of smoky Chardonnay; the chocolate mousse; the
mango slices; the turkish coffee; the exotic pungent smell
of my father's Havana cigar. It had all been too rich and
plentiful. I had vomited most of it in the men's washroom,
and did not mention this to my father when I returned to

the table with mottled face and pounding heart. I would let nothing mar the indescribable joy of sharing a meal as the privileged guest of this very special man.

To my left, as I turned to walk along the beach, I could see the same old timber pier jutting out to sea, with its unevenly tilted boardwalk distorted over the years by the irregular subsidence of the stanchions into the sandy seabed. Two fishermen were sitting on folding canvas stools at the end of the pier, preparing their tackle and moving in slow motion. Fishing, I reflected, is a leisurely pursuit — except deep sea fishing, which is more like big game hunting.

I walked toward the pier and sat on the sand in the cool shade beneath. Another aroma was added to the perfumes of the sea: ancient timbers pickled by the salt water. The silvery sun-baked pine of the boardwalk above me and the barnacle encrusted wetness of the partially submerged pillars around me were shedding essences that recreated vividly for me the day when my father and I had lingered on that very same spot. I stood up and noticed a small black crab scamper out of sight to the other side of the stanchion. *'Listen, I threw pebbles at your ancestors when I was a little boy'* I called out, *'I see that legend has been handed down to you. Take care of yourself, do you hear?'*

As I walked away from the pier, my footsteps leaving their prints on the moist sand hardened by the receding tide, I heard a snapping sound as one of the fishermen flicked the cap off a lemonade bottle against the edge of his metal kit-box and remembered how clearly sound can carry across water. I stretched out my arms and took a deep breath and realized that it was not the shapes and colours and muted sounds of my surroundings that brought the images I recalled into such sharp focus. No, it was the perfumes of the sea, and those had been my father's words. The air I

breathed in slowly and tasted had been seasoned with the
salts of the sea and enriched with the vapours of corals and
essences of living things. It carried the microscopic fuses
that fired my memory at long-hidden targets, releasing
scenes preserved in clearest detail from the locked vaults
of my mind.

*   *   *

*'Even Emperors and lesser Masters of the Universe have
discovered an important fact at the moment of death'. . .*
those words now appeared on my mind's horizon as I sat
at the water's edge, the surf breaking over my legs and
cooling me in the early afternoon sun. The waves were
gradually pulling a little sand out from under me each time
they retreated, creating a shallow pool in which I wallowed
dreamily, rocked into distant musings by the ebb and flow
of the ocean. . .

I was thinking about the time, only a few years earlier,
when my father and I were spending two weeks on
Eleuthera — a Bahamian island ten miles long and one
mile across at its widest point. At its narrowest point, a
mere twenty foot wide neck of land separated the Caribbean
from the Atlantic Ocean and it was the contrast between the
oceans that had drawn us back to the same spot day after
day.

We would often stand for a long while where we could see,
a few feet to our left, the clear calm turquoise waters of the
warm Caribbean, with its sandy bottom clearly visible and,
only a few feet away on our right, the deep, cold and dark
blue turbulent Atlantic beating menacingly against the
rocks. It seemed as though a whole continent had been
mysteriously removed from between the two seas, leaving

only a narrow strip of land barely wide enough for the tarred road that ran along the length of the island. The view fascinated us and it became an allegory in our minds for other contrasts that had affected both our lives in the past.

My father had occasionally been preoccupied and melancholy during our stay on the island. I had found it disturbing, at first, to be lying on a sandy beach in the sunshine listening to my father talking about life. . . and death. . . an event that was somehow out of place in those surroundings. Was the Angel of Death always pictured reaping his harvest of lives in the sinister twilit gloom of an overcast sky — man's expression of the universal fear of death, the morbid imagery of the most terrible taboo of all? Why not in the sunshine? It might make the prospect of dying a little less frightening. . . with a cheerful comforting guide to lead one out. On the other hand, I concluded, perhaps that wasn't such a good idea. I had once seen bright sunshine and death joined together on the sands of war.

I had been worried for some time that the old man might be planning to end his life. . . he would go about it carefully and would no doubt carry it out thoughtfully, even elegantly, knowing my father's consideration for others and his unwavering observance of decorous behaviour. I felt that he would want to be the one to decide on the circumstances and the date of his departure from this world. He had been trounced too often by chance throughout his life and maybe he had it in mind to cheat chance of that ultimate victory over him. He would, of course, have been aware of the lack of logic in his reasoning, but the notion would appeal to him all the same. On the other hand, had my anxiety, I wondered, been leading me deceptively along the wrong road into his thoughts?

Whatever my own reasoning may have been, there was still a fear that would not recede. One morning, as we were lying on the beach, I drew a deep breath and said to him: "You know, Katsuo once told me that self-knowledge comes to you at the precise moment when you are about to end your life by your own hand — because suicide is the only thing in your life over which you have complete control. Well, I don't know about that. Oh, of course it has a morbidly grandiose ring to it, but I disagree simply because it is inaccurate: we do also have it in our complete control to make others happy or miserable"

I knew I had made my point because the old man gave me an oblique reply: "Yes, but you should realize that even Emperors and lesser Masters of the Universe have discovered an important fact at the moment of death. . . oh yes, they may have attendants and courtiers, slaves, relatives, wives and concubines and all their children by their side, with the multitude beyond the palace gates howling and tearing their garments with grief. . . it makes little difference because they know one thing for sure: it is only when you are about to die that you are truly alone. You see, it's not something in which anyone can join, even if they are holding your hand or a loving lip is on yours when the moment arrives"

I knew that my father believed he was rapidly approaching the end of his days and I was disturbed by his remarks. He had not set my mind at rest. I replied: "Yes, but if they love you, are they not sharing with you. . . I mean, helping you to face the loss of the most precious thing. . ."

He interrupted me in that quietly obstinate way of his: "Yes, maybe. But for me, dying is the most private act of all, and I would prefer to be alone when it happens. You look hurt. . . don't be my dear son. . . because you know that a desire for privacy is not an uncaring gesture, and it should not be paid for with remorse over the wounded feelings of others. My love for you will not, at the very end, demand your presence. Remember that, and be comforted"

"But Papa! How can I be comforted by what you have said? Surely when the time comes, my presence and Maman's should be a matter for *us* to decide. Are we offered no choice?" I asked him reproachfully.

He turned and looked at me with his pale blue eyes magnified by the thick-lensed glasses he wore: "Of course you have a choice my boy. . . but there are many things we humans prefer to do in solitude, and I imagine you would have no desire to intrude upon these, would you? . ."

He was very determined, I could see, and I had no wish to contradict him. "No, I understand what you mean. . . I suppose what you said. . . it just caught me by surprise. . ."

My father paused for a while, sitting cross-legged, silently smoothing the sand in front of him with the palm of his hand. He then gathered small seashells and started to form a snowflake pattern with them, from the centre outward. I joined him in the exercise, and when we had finished, the design had grown to almost three feet in diameter. It was a beautiful creative work of flawless radial symmetry and we both burst out laughing — as humans do when they have accomplished something clever — and then we waded slowly into the warm ocean.

When we returned to the beach, it was clear that the old man had held on to the thread of his earlier train of thought: "We humans find only one thing worse than the threat of death: and that's the prospect of everlasting uncertainty. Why else do you think that some men in death cells wish desperately to be executed without delay. . . and beg their defenders to stop obtaining reprieve after reprieve after they themselves have given up hope? It's like being subjected to a grisly cycle of death and resurrection endlessly repeated. . . and yet we are expected to believe that a benevolent God condemned his Son to a resurrection! It makes the Christ's sacrificial death utterly pointless. Why can't they see that? And what father would condemn his own son to a slow death in a mood of frustrated pique so as to make the creatures he created feel guilty enough to start behaving the way he wants them to. . . while knowing all along that he'd bring the boy back to life anyway? Et bien, ce serait un père ignoble et bien capricieux. Oh, the ancient Greek and Indian poets could dream up some gruesome gods. . . but this one beats them all. It's those people who can still worship this kind of ghoulish deity who are hard for me to understand. . . and I happen to know several charming little old ladies who believe it's about time their God did something about all the horrid people in the world. It frightens me to think what they have in mind. Now Jesus wanted to die. It was his decision. He wasn't the first to want that, and he won't be the last. . . and Christians have cheated him for almost two thousand years by cursing him with a resurrection he never wanted. David, in his twenty-second Psalm, sang: *My God, my God, why hast thou forsaken me?* And then started his twenty-third Psalm with the words: *The Lord is my shepherd; I shall not want.* But Jesus only cried out the first words of the twenty-second Psalm. And then he died, poor lad. I daresay he was tired of it all"

The question of the Resurrection obviously troubled my father and created profound doubts in his spiritual thinking. It must also have raised still more questions which remained unanswered, because those questions eventually brought his belief in the Supreme Being to a standstill. I am reminded of that part of the prayer, in his early

treasured copy of *'The Works of William Paley, Doctor of
Divinity, Published in 1825'*, that he underlined in pencil
and which I found among his possessions — as well as the
puzzling note I discovered tucked inside the book, neatly
written in my father's firm spidery copperplate style.

THE CLERGYMAN'S COMPANION
A Prayer of Preparation for Death

*O Almighty God, Maker and Judge of all men, have mercy
upon me, thy weak and sinful creature; and if by thy most
wise and righteous appointment the hour of death be
approaching towards me, enable me to meet it with a mind
fully prepared for it, and to pass through this great and
awful trial in the manner most profitable to me. . . . And,
O merciful Father, give me that supply of spiritual comfort,
which thou seest needful for me in my present condition:
and grant that, when my change comes, I may die with a
quiet conscience, with a well-grounded assurance of thy
favor, and a joyful hope of a blessed resurrection; through
our Lord and Saviour Jesus Christ. Amen.*

My father's note says: *And we thank thee, Almighty God,
for thy great gift of the English Language, without which
we would doubtless be deprived of the well-grounded
assurance of thy favour and the joyful hope of a blessed
resurrection, but just possibly still die profitably with a
clear conscience.*

The old man had, it seemed to me, developed an irreverent
sense of irony somewhere along the way.

$$* \qquad * \qquad *$$

I remember now another day on the beach terrace in
Eleuthera. We were breakfasting on chilled papaya spiced

with fresh lime juice followed by broiled grouper steaks. The steaks were delicious, but we had both eaten only a mouthful when we had looked at each other and wordlessly pushed our plates to one side. Why did we do that? . . Some sentimental anthropomorphic hang-up? Yes, perhaps. We had swum out the day before to a lone submerged rock jutting out of the sandy seabed about sixty feet from the shore. With our diving masks we could see that the rock was no more than about ten feet in diameter. . . but every inch of it, every little crevice, had been colonized by a countless variety of marine creatures. Coelenterates of every kind formed a colourful tapestry on the rock face: cup polyps, anemones, sea firs and sea pens, all competing with one another for space on that miniature coral condominium. It was an underwater oasis in an arid desert of golden sand, brightly lit by the sun's rays in an unclouded crystal sea.

Swimming lazily round the rock were dozens of small brightly disguised coral reef fishes in orbit. . . then Gorgeous Gussy the Grouper! She was *BIG*. The solitary Great Empress of that microcosmic universe. . . and nosey. She got in the way. . . she made a nuisance of herself. . . she nudged us until we stroked her large silvery white belly, and then she would tilt at an angle of ten degrees to show her appreciation. Sentimental maybe. . . but try eating grouper steak after *that!*

So we ordered poached eggs on toast and tried to rid our minds of thoughts of cannibalism as we sipped our coffee. My father lit his pipe and, looking out toward the ocean, said: "You know son, I do believe that life's objective uselessness is what gives it grandeur. The only thing which is likely to ensure the survival of life on this planet is efficient management — not moral postures. Our own lives are so exquisitely provisional that it requires a great imaginative leap to concern ourselves with the survival — let alone the comfort — of distantly future generations. It is only if we see it as an expedient duty to ourselves, that we are likely to take action to preserve this planet for our descendants"

That evening, as we were having an early dinner, I remarked to the old man, for no apparent reason that I can recall: "You know Dad, I really always believed you were the wisest person in the world. . . no, what I'm trying to say. . . look, it's not that I. . ." And he smiled wisely as he interrupted me: "No, son, no need to explain. . . listen, no single person has a monopoly on wisdom and it's a bad mistake to float in the slipstream of another person's thoughts, like a sycamore seed rotating weightlessly in mid-air and never touching the ground. John Locke and Buddha and quite a few others through the ages have said: *'Look at the facts and think for yourself'*. Why do people need constant reminding? Listen son, there is no single way to achieve wisdom: it's not a state that can be reached at some journey's end. The ultimate beatitude doesn't exist and it is cruelly irresponsible to put it on offer. . . to raise false hopes. . . because it diminishes and spoils the full enjoyment, the appreciation and the understanding of life as well as its pleasure and its pain, in full measure. It is a tragedy to discover this too late in life, when the sweet seed corn has shrivelled to nothing, and only the dry chaff remains. The greatest enemy of truth, my dear boy, is self-deception"

Later that evening, over a glass of brandy, I used the word *freedom,* I cannot remember the context, but I do remember part of the old man's reply: "Yes of course, but freedom's limit is the line which must be drawn where another person's freedom is affected". And although I cannot recall why he did so, later in the conversation he asked the rhetorical question: "So, my boy. . . would you set a canary free?"

I also remember a fragment of our conversation on the plane as we were flying home. My father said: "Yes, we all carry within us the instinct to kill for self protection, but we suppress it. . . most of the time we don't go around blasting one another to kingdom come. But there are other ways of killing. . . that's when we want someone out of the way. We want very sick people and very dirty people out of the way, and we sometimes want obstreperous and mad people and people who disagree with us out of the way. But we can't admit, ever, that we could wish them dead, because the guilt and the shame would be unbearable. So we turn away. . . we turn our backs on these people. And, because we all have good in us, we find ways to justify this method of obliterating those we believe to be a threat to our peace of mind. We kill without guilt when we practice indifference"

A month later the old man caught pneumonia and as he was being carried out of the house on a stretcher on his way to hospital he turned to me with a smile and said in French: "Go and find my pince-nez, my little one. . . I can't see the time without them and I fear I am late"

A few weeks after, in a small desk drawer in his study, I found the old pince-nez he had not worn for almost forty years, as well as a photograph of a small boy.

Then I suddenly remembered that small boy's dream of becoming a storyteller, like the old Travelling Teller of Tales, and realised that I should now make that dream come true.

Glossary of Foreign Vernacular Words

Most of the slang words or expressions are translated into the nearest English equivalent.

Language Key: **[A]** Arabic   **[I]** Italian
              [F] French   **[J]** Japanese

Absolument fada [F]: absolutely daft; idiotic.

Affreets [A]: devils; evil spirits.

Al fresco [F]: out of doors (origin: Italian).

Anah Hinah [A]: I am here.

Après tout [F]: after all.

Au naturel [F]: unadorned (i.e. naked).

Au revoir mes chers amis [F]: goodbye my dear friends.

Badaoui [A]: Bedouin.

Ba'lawa [A]: a flaky pastry cake filled with nuts, fruit and syrup.

Beurre noire [F]: butter browned in the pan and used in certain dishes.

Bien difficile [F]: pretty difficult; awkward.

Bien entendu [F]: needless to say.

Blanqette d'agneau [F]: lamb casserole with cream, seasoned with lemon.

Bon Dieu [F]: good God.

Bookrah fi'l mishmish [A]: very unlikely to happen; never in a month of Sundays.

Bourrique [F]: an ass; a stubborn ignoramus.

Canaille [F]: a scoundrel.

Caneur [F]: yellow belly; coward.

Ce petit cochon [F]: that little pig.

Ce p'tit bonhomme [F]: that little man.

Ce serait un père ignoble et bien capricieux [F]: it would be an unworthy and freakish father.

C'est ignoble [F]: it's unworthy; base.

C'est vraiment tragique [F]: it's really tragic.

Chadana [J]: a cabinet in which tea utensils are kept.

Chaude pisse [F]: the clap; gonorrhoea.

Commendatore [I]: a title generally awarded for civic merit and often used loosely as a sign of respect.

Conduite atroce [F]: appalling behaviour.

Conneries [F]: crap; bloody nonsense.

Con pomodoro [I]: with potatoes.

Cracheur [F]: big-head; swank.

Crise de nerfs [F]: a fit of hysteria.

Dégueulasse [F]: sickening; disgusting.

Dejà vu [F]: the illusion of experiencing in an identical way something that happened before.

Derrière [F]: backside; rear; bum.

Deus misereatur [F]: the canticle God be merciful.

Dieu du ciel [F]: God in heaven above.

Dio mio! [I]: My God!

Donc j'éspère que vous comprenez ce que je veux dire [F]: hence I trust you understand what I mean.

Emmerdeur [F]: a bloody nuisance.

Empapaouté [F]: a poof; an effeminate man.

En brosse [F]: like a brush (a crew-cut hair style).

En tout les cas [F]: in any case.

Et bien [F]: well then.

Excessivement pénible [F]: extremely painful.

Fagot [F]: a queer; a homosexual.

Fais bien attention [F]: take great care; be very careful.

Fanatique [F]: a fanatic.

Farceur [F]: a practical joker; a humbug; a faker.

Fellahin [A]: peasant labourers.

Foutrement con [F]: bloody ridiculous.

Foutu a la porte [F]: chucked out; slung out of the door.

Fripouillard [F]: a trickster; a con man.

Ghallabeya [A]: a plain long cotton robe with flared sleeves, worn by males.

Gros plein de soupe [F]: (fat man full of soup); great fat lump; self-important wealthy man.

Hai [J]: yes.

Haramlek [A]: the harem; the womens' quarters.

Hibachi [J]: a charcoal burner or small stove.

Iftaahe ya Simsim [A]: Open, oh Sesame.

Il a très bon coeur après tout [F]: he is kind hearted, after all.

Incroyable [F]: incredible.

Insupportable [F]: unbearable.

Ishtah [A]: cream from milk.

Jardin d'éden céleste [F]: celestial Garden of Eden.

Je vous en supplie [F]: I beg you.

Jouer de la mandoline [F]: (to play the mandolin); to masturbate.

Khamseen [A]: a sandstorm.

Kohl [A]: a dark powder made from antimony, used to darken eyelids.

Konafa [A]: a sweet bun made from fine strands of pastry.

Kubbebas [A]: oval spiced meatballs stuffed with pine kernels and herbs.

Kuftas [A]: minced lamb meatballs, usually grilled on skewers.

La peur bleue d'une malheureuse circoncision [F]: blue funk (fear) of an accidental circumcision.

Lei mi dice una cosa cattivella in Inglese [I]: You're saying something a little naughty to me in English.

Les demoiselles [F]: the young ladies.

Louche [F]: suspect; dodgy

Macaronis [F]: penises.

Ma cosa posso fare io co questo poltrone [I]: what can I do with this lazy villain.

Madonna Santa [I]: Sainted Madonna.

Ma foie [F]: upon my faith; gracious me.

Mais alors [F]: well then.

Maison close [F]: a brothel.

Mais vous êtes complètement fou [F]: but you are quite mad.

Medlars [A]: small apple-like fruit eaten when blet (over–ripe).

Merci beaucoup [F]: thank you very much.

Merde alors [F]: damn it all.

Mes enfants [F]: my children.

Met'shakkir jiddan [A]: thank you very much; much obliged.

Missa cantata [F]: the choirbook of Catholic Mass.

Mon [J]: a family crest or coat of arms.

Mon vieux [F]: old boy (affectionate term)

Nabboot [A]: a long wooden stave.

Non con semolina per l'amor di Dio [I]: not with semolina, for the love of God.

Non pareil [F]: unique; beyond compare.

Notre Dame Du Sacré Coeur Sanglant de Jésus [F]: Our Lady of the Sacred Bleeding Heart of Jesus.

Nubian [A]: a native of Nubia, now an area of northern Sudan.

Oni [J]: a small mischievous devil; a gremlin.

Palais [F]: palace.

Par dessus le marché [F]: Moreover

Parthians [A]: natives of an ancient kingdom in western Asia.

Petite hysterie [F]: minor hysteria.

Petit Salaud [F]: dirty little beast.

Petit Sauvage [F]: little savage.

Pourquoi pas [F]: why not.

Privé de la parole [F]: speechless.

Que cattivo [I]: what a naughty man.

Rab'binna Khal'leek [A]: may God preserve you; God bless you.

Raisonnable [F]: reasonable; sensible.

Ramadan [A]: the ninth month of the Muslim calendar; the month of fasting by daytime.

Ravissant [F]: ravishing; perfectly splendid.

Salamlek [A]: the king's quarters and reception rooms.

Sashimi [J]: portions of sliced raw fish.

Sharbaat [A]: sweet beverages.

Si j'ose dire [F]: I dare say.

Soirées [F]: social evening gatherings.

Soit disant [F]: so called.

Sumi-e [J]: painting in black ink.

Tahina [A]: sesame seed paste.

Tantine [F]: Aunt (affectionate term).

Tanuki-Bozu [J]: a legendary badger disguised as a priest.

Tatami [J]: a reed floor mat.

Tisane [F]: a herbal infusion.

Tokonoma [J]: an alcove in a home where certain objects are kept for worship or aesthetic appreciation.

Torch cul [F]: arse-wiper (toilet tissue).

Tordant [F]: hilarious.

Tromperie [F]: an act of infidelity (or deceitfulness).

Tu [F]: thou (more intimate than 'vous').

Tu comprends [F]: you understand.

Un Boche [F]: a Gerry (a German).

Une inconvenance insupportable [F]: an unbearable impropriety.

Une véritable révélation [F]: a true revelation.

Un supplice éternel [F]: an unending torment.

Vierge [F]: virgin.

Vieux couillon [F]: silly old bugger.

Votre conduite est incompréhensible [F]: your behaviour is beyond understanding.

Vous [F]: you.

Vous verrez [F]: you'll see.

Voyons donc [F]: now then, let's be reasonable.

Wasabi [J]: Japanese green horseradish.

Wazir [A]: State Minister; High Councillor.

Ya Bey [A]: sir or sire; (originally: your highness).

Ya din el Nabi! [A]: By the Prophet's Faith!

Ya habibtee [A]: my sweetheart.

Zaraats [A]: farts.

About the Author

Michael Henry Birch was born in Egypt of Anglo-French parentage and has often been in the right place at the right time (or the wrong one depending on one's point of view).

In World War II he occasionally played the organ in a house of ill-repute in Cairo, the piano once in a jam session with members of the Glenn Miller Band and was a private in the United States Army Air Forces.

After the war he was a tap-dancing chorus boy in a London theatre and a late night cabaret artist. He drank with Dylan Thomas in Bloomsbury, threw pots for Picasso in Vallauris, and was mildly praised by Henry Moore in Camberwell.

He married in 1948 and washed dishes at Lyon's Corner House. Later he worked as a telephone operator at the International Exchange in London. After that he designed spectacle frames but was sacked by his last employer in 1954 and then went on to found an international group of industrial companies. He retired from the business world at the age of forty-four after, he claims, it had lost its charm.

He became a professional carver of Japanese netsuke, held his first one man show at the Eskenazi Gallery in London in 1976, and was designated Master Carver by the Japanese artists' guild. His work is now represented in the major international collections. He has been a writer for the past five years and *The Teller of Tall Tales* is the first of his books to be published.

J.K.L.G.